THE PRACTICAL DREAMER
and Other Stories to Tell at Christmas

The PRACTICAL DREAMER

AND OTHER STORIES TO TELL AT

CHRISTMAS

RICHARD P. OLSON

UPPER ROOM BOOKS

NASHVILLE

The Practical Dreamer
and Other Stories to Tell at Christmas

Cover design: Jim Bateman
Book design: Nancy Johnstone
First printing: September 1990 (7)
Second printing: July 1991 (3)
Third printing: August 1992 (3)
ISBN 0-8358-0611-1
Library of Congress Card Number: 89-51766

Printed in the United States of America

This book is dedicated to:

Two grandchildren, Daniel and Carolyn—
May they be "children of peace,"

And to three congregations:
First Baptist Church of Racine, Wisconsin
First Baptist Church of Boulder, Colorado
Prairie Baptist Church, Prairie Village, Kansas

These churches received these stories and
encouraged the stories. Together, we celebrated
the story.

CONTENTS

TWELVE WAYS TO CHRISTMAS:
A FOREWORD

One way to describe Advent is that it is a journey toward the stable and manger in which Jesus was born. While Advent includes many other themes and images as well, it is at least that journey toward Bethlehem we make each year with Mary and Joseph. Our primary guides on the trip are Matthew and Luke, the two gospel writers who take time to tell of Jesus' birth.

In this book Richard Olson has followed the lead of those gospel writers in offering some additional paths along which to make our way toward Christmas. In fact, he describes a dozen different ways to Bethlehem, journeys his congregation has taken with him on past Christmas Eves.

Olson's stories do something else, though, something that may be just as important. They serve as examples of gifts each of us might give to our congregations, classes, or families. Certainly we can read (or better yet, tell) the stories contained here. But we might also view them as starting places from which we might make our own journeys and tell our own stories.

The strength of these twelve retellings of the Christmas story is that instead of trying to explain to us what the birth of Jesus "means," they allow us to *experience* that world-changing event as if we were there. When we retell our version of the Nativity, we can create a similar experience for our listeners. As we do, persons of all ages and backgrounds can hear the glad tidings that were intended for all the people.

How do we begin to tell the glad tidings? We can start with the aspect of stories called "point of view." In other words, over whose shoulder will we be looking as we enter the world of the story? Who will be directing our attention to what is important in that world? Olson offers a number of examples: three strangers who meet in an inn, Joseph, two mothers—one Soviet and one American—and their children, a visitor from another planet, and even the earth itself.

Once you have chosen the character—ancient or modern, real or imagined—with whom you will make the journey to Christmas, ask how that person experiences the world of the story. What will she or he see, hear, smell, taste, or touch? What other characters will that character encounter? How will that character feel and think about the other persons and events in the world created by your story? You may wish to jot down some notes as images and ideas come to you.

Where will your story take place? In the stable, on the way to or from that place, in a home or church, in your home country, or another part of the world? *When* will your story take place? At the time of Jesus' birth, today, or even tomorrow?

Once you have thought through the point of view, place, and time, you may wish to outline an order of events. When you have the flow of the story in mind, you are ready to write or tell it. Whether you prepare your story in a written or oral form, you will want to practice it until it becomes a part of you and you can tell it to your family, class, or congregation.

As Mordecai tells his new-found friends in "Three Strangers," "we are bound together by a story." We are, indeed, bound together by a story. Each time we tell it from our various traditions and personal experiences our voices blend into a harmony that, different as we are, binds us together with each other, the Christ we follow, and the God we worship. May every Advent find us each on a fresh journey to Christmas, telling each other what we have seen along the way.

MICHAEL E. WILLIAMS

INTRODUCTION

During an Advent, about a dozen years ago, I attempted a modest innovation.

Story had always been an important part of Advent and Christmas for me. In my childhood church, my minister frequently shared a beloved Christmas story in one of the worship services of the season. In my ministry, I had attempted the same thing—to tell the stories of Christmas and about Christmas in some way. Stories such as "The Other Wise Man" and "Why the Chimes Rang" were favorites that I had both heard and told. However, sometimes these stories didn't quite fit the need, setting, timing, or schedule of the congregations I served.

So one year, with some fear and hesitation, I decided to write a Christmas story myself and tell it on Christmas Eve. This was such a lovely, exhilarating experience for me—and for the congregation also, it seemed—that I have continued it. With few exceptions, I have written one story each year since.

This writing of a Christmas story each year has at least three strands: It is part of my Advent devotion and discipline; it is a Christmas gift to myself; and it is a Christmas gift to the congregation. I find it impossible to separate those three strands. For me, writing these stories is one of those marvelous places where discipline and joy meet.

This volume contains most of those once-a-year Christmas stories that I have written and told. Most of them focus on the Nativity and Advent scriptures, while a few are contemporary reflections. There is, of course, a fair amount of repetition in them. After all, there are only four chapters of the Bible that speak of these matters at all.

However, writing these stories has increasingly revealed the richness of those scriptural narratives to me. To use a photographer's metaphor, I have varied my focus from wide angle to telephoto to microscopic. The stories are told from various perspectives: shortly after it happened, a generation or two later, or from our twentieth-century perspective. A story's source may be the account from Luke or Matthew. Or, in concert with prevailing practice, it might combine them. Each person, each location, each detail has a mystery behind it, and the storyteller probes those for beauty and insight.

Although some of the stories include, as accurately as possible, historical biblical detail, others are mostly the product of my imagination. All of them reveal more about the storyteller's encounter with the Christmas story than they do about that story itself. Some of them were written to illuminate my congregation's issues and questions, and others were expressive of my life journey. Shortly after I became a grandparent for the first time, my daughter told me that year's story was a "grandpa story." I think she is right.

After writing these stories for years, I heard that a teacher of creative writing told his students that it is impossible to write a new or original Christmas story! This may be true. It is possible, however, to spend time with an old friend and discover some things that one had passed by earlier. Those scripture passages in Matthew 1–2 and Luke 1–2 are just such old friends that may hold new treasures for each of us.

These stories are now offered to you in the hope that they will serve you in many ways. If you enjoy them and find them entertaining, that is great. If they stir wonder and awe, that is even better. If you'd like to tell one to a group or at a worship service, I will be honored. However, if you find yourself saying, "That's interesting, but I think he missed the point. The way I visualize this story is . . . "—that will be best of all.

To me, it seems faithful not only to tell those matchless stories, but to express my response in story. Such may be fact or fiction. If the story expresses honest conviction and belief, it is true! Scholars are now using the term "narrative theology" to describe the style of expressing convictions and beliefs through narrative and story, rather than (or in addition to) propositions and discourse. In this, they are but discovering the way of Jesus and of many Old Testament writers before his time.

I invite you to join me in approaching the Christmas story with a child's curiosity and imagination. Ask yourself many questions, such as: How do I visualize this event? What were the people thinking and feeling when it happened? What did this event mean to them? What does it mean to me? In the brief biblical telling, what details were omitted? What other things happened that the Bible writer did not include? If someone walked down the street today living out this Bible truth, what would it look like?

Live with such questions. When one strikes a spark, sit down and begin to write a story about it. Don't worry that you don't know how it will turn out. My experience is that once begun, stories sometimes take on a life of their own and tell themselves.

I once heard Jesus described as the poet who makes poets of us all. To me, he is the storyteller who makes storytellers of us all. He is the story that calls forth story in us. For, of all the wonderful tales he told, only one exceeds in fascination—the story of his coming. For generations, millions of us storytellers have told and will continue to tell about "when Jesus was born in Bethlehem of Judea in the days of Herod the King." At the end of time, we will not have exhausted its meaning.

THREE STRANGERS

The night was dark and overcast, damp and chilly. A noisy wind blew eerily around houses and down narrow roads. This darkness was all the deeper in the gloomy, winding streets of Bethlehem. Two men hurried down the street toward each other, unaware of the other's presence. They pulled their garments up over their heads for protection and warmth as they made their way down the alley-like little lane.

Suddenly they collided. Both thought they had been attacked and grabbed for their weapons. One drew a Roman sword from the sheath at his side, the other a short dagger from the cord that held his inner garment. They stood, tensed, staring into the darkness. Slowly each made out the other's figure, standing totally surprised. As no attack followed the first collision, they sensed it had been an accident. Warily watching the other, each returned his weapon to its place. Without speaking, they nodded to each other and turned to go. But they moved in the same direction, down side streets. Shortly, both arrived at the same place, a small inn, the only place for a drink and some warmth in this tiny town on such a forbidding night.

As they stepped into the serving room of the inn, the light was still dim and flickering, but brighter than outside. The room was chilly, but less cold than outdoors. They lowered their garments from around their heads and looked at each other. The larger man was a Roman centurion. His name was Artemus. The thinner, shorter, wiry man was an Arab shepherd. His name was Ishmael.

Their eyes turned to the room they had entered. Though the rest of Bethlehem had seemed deserted, this place was not! It was filled with people who were drinking, talking, laughing, gaming. There seemed to be nowhere to sit. From the far end of the room, they saw an older man sitting at a small table by himself. Squinting, he looked toward them and vaguely waved his hand, beckoning Artemus and Ishmael. Each took the invitation to be for himself, and so each made his way by separate routes, pushing between crowded benches, stepping around bodies. At about the same time, both arrived at the partially empty table of the older man. He was stocky but not fat, with a tinge of gray in both his hair and beard. This man, the innkeeper, was a Jew by the name of Mordecai. He had seen dimly that some customers had come in and had no place to sit, and so he was a bit surprised when two quite different persons arrived at his table. Wordlessly he gestured to both of them to be seated, and they did.

Without speaking to one another, each ordered his drink and sipped his hot wine in silence, holding the large cup close for added warmth. Most of the time they looked down into their cups; but occasionally their eyes met uneasily, and the silence seemed strained. Three men who would never meet socially were crowded at a little table. They were uncomfortable, but did not know what to do.

Ishmael was an outgoing man who did not like silence. It was he who first spoke. Turning to Artemus he asked, "How's the occupation going?"

"Tense and troubled, as you well know," Artemus barked. Then realizing that in his usual fashion he was sounding much more harsh than he intended, he explained, "You know, all of us dread assignment to

Judea. Oh, you have a beautiful land. But it's so difficult here. Other places where I've been don't like to be ruled by Rome either. But here, it's as if the people are never conquered. There is always something stirring. Sometimes you feel it deep inside and don't know where even to start looking. It's like we Romans are violating . . . God, or something! I hope I'm not here when the revolution comes. It will be a battle to the end. For we are just here on assignment, but these people fight in the name of their God for everything they believe in and stand for."

Mordecai and Ishmael looked at each other, surprised to hear such sentiments from a respected Roman centurion. They relaxed a bit. Mordecai asked, "Is the census finished?"

Speaking a bit too loudly, Artemus responded, "Yes, and what a fool's errand that was!" Looking about to be sure he was not overheard by any fellow Romans, Artemus continued, speaking more quietly. "I will give Quirinius credit for a stroke of genius for having each of them go to the city of their ancestors. That seemed to touch some feeling of national pride so that the resistance wasn't as bad as feared. It was strange, at the census. People standing in line would be hugging each other, laughing, playing. Then when they got to the desk for the census report and tax, they would be angry and sullen. Some would spit, narrowly missing the census taker. Others would refuse payment till we held them and took it from them, kicking and screaming. A few would be so arrogant that we would have to give them a bit of a whipping. But let me tell you about the strangest one of all!" Mordecai and Ishmael leaned close. Artemus exclaimed, "One man laughed! Yes, that's true. I was in the interrogating seat when he came and I asked, 'How many people do you register?' 'Two that you can count,' he said, and burst out laughing. I asked him again, and he responded the same way with another peal of laughter. Then I saw his wife standing, waiting for him. She was very, very pregnant. I smiled as if I understood. I could see that a yet unborn child would escape the census tax, but there must be more to it than that! At that point she spoke, 'Joseph, please hurry.' He immediately supplied the information and promptly paid the tax. Then they were on their way, tenderly walking with arms around each other. Like I said before, there's always something going on inside these people. How can you ever conquer a country when the people laugh at your taxes? I'd give anything to know what happened to that young couple."

"I can tell you," Mordecai responded. "They came to my inn." Artemus looked up in surprise. Mordecai continued. "They came in at the peak of the rush. I wish you Romans could time things better. Too little business . . . then too much business . . . then too little business . . . I was doing my best to deal with the huge crowds. With all your taxes and demands, it's such a struggle to make a living." He seemed to be blaming Artemus for all that Rome did. They drew back from each other, but Mordecai went on. "I was trying to make a few extra shekels. Then this young man appeared, pleading for a place for his wife—by now in labor—and himself. I'm not a cruel man, but business is business. I had no room, and even if I had, he couldn't pay what I can ask when there is a crowd in town. While I was explaining this, they caught my wife's eye. She's too soft to be in business. She said she'd work something out and led them away. I immediately turned to the next customer and thought no more of it, what with the rush and all.

"But then as that long and hard evening wore on, I sensed something strange going on. My wife, my daughter who was helping, or my servant women would disappear from time to time. Nowhere could I find them. And then shortly they'd be there, with smiles for everyone. They'd rush about, eager to please, showing no sign of the tiredness I was feeling in every bone. I was puzzled. In a rare moment when no one was asking for anything, I took my wife aside and asked what was going on. She whispered, 'I put the young couple up in a corner of one of the caves where we stable the animals. She's delivered a son!' Then I understood where they'd been. Women can't resist peeking at a baby. But if it cheered them through the long night, what did I care? About an hour later I stepped outside for a breath of air, and without realizing it, my steps took me toward that cave, where—I'll admit it, like a woman—I peeked in. The husband welcomed me, warmly thanked me for *my* caring hospitality (fancy that!), and led me to the wife and child. I returned often through the night, drawn as if by a magnet. In between times, I'd try to make my inn a place of hospitality. The money didn't matter so much anymore. But I *looked* for those moments to return to the manger, to the quiet power, the love, the peace that was there."

At the word *peace* Ishmael perked up and eagerly responded. "Yes, that's it," he said, "but it wasn't any ordinary peace. You see, I saw the child, too."

Mordecai and Artemus turned their attention to the wiry, talkative little Arab shepherd. But it took him a moment to continue. He seemed to be struggling within himself, wanting to share a favorite secret, but at the same time feeling afraid of being laughed at. In time, with unaccustomed hesitancy, he began. "I've never believed in ghosts or spirits or even an unseen God. What I see, that's what I believe! I'm not one of those fancy minds that imagines lots of things. If anyone told me what I'm going to tell you, I'd think he'd gone off, touched in the head. I swear what I am going to say is true. Up on shepherd's hill the other night, it turned day in the middle of the night. Bright, *bright* day! Hurt your eyes. All of us were scared, but I wanted to know what was going on; so I looked straight at the light while the others hid their heads. I saw messengers in the light. I heard music like I'd never coaxed out of my pipes. I heard voices—voices talking about not being afraid (fat chance!) and about joyous news for all people (being Arab, I liked that part about *all* people). Then there was something about a savior being born, and the way we'd know it was we'd find a baby in a cave! Then it was over. Well, all of us who were off duty rushed off. A baby in a cave would be something we could see, something we didn't expect to find. But sure enough, there they were. Just like the messenger in the middle of the day in the middle of the night had said. You were right, Mordecai. There was *peace* in that manger. But it wasn't just any kind of peace that folks like you and me can make. I only believe what I can see, and I saw peace in those people!"

Mordecai looked up with amazement. "I thought we were strangers. I only waved you over here because I didn't want to lose your business. But now we are bound together by a story." And he reached out in a three-way embracing handshake of the other two, clutching wrists and arms. It was the warmest expression he had ever made to an Arab or a Roman.

Then they leaned back on their benches, quietly thinking. "I wish they had not gone away," said Mordecai. "I miss them."

Artemus responded, "I think we will hear from them again. When we do, I hope it will be good news for each of us."

Ishmael quietly said, "It will be."

By now the last few remaining lamps were burning out of oil. The inn was practically empty. They rose to go.

"*Pax*," said the Roman.

"*Shalom*," said the Jew.

"*Salaam*," said the Arab.

And for those with ears to hear, there was in and beyond the wind, one last refrain of a song that will never be forgotten: "Glory to God in the highest, and on earth peace, good will toward all."

THE PEACE WARRIOR

I was stunned but excited by the announcement I heard. Yet I knew I must think clearly and quickly to gain the most from this unusual opportunity.

I was part of a select group of fifteen journalists who had been invited to this consultation. Each of us had been covering various aspects of the peace movement for years. I must admit that I was a rather tired, cynical reporter by then.

For months we had heard rumors that we were to be afforded a very special opportunity, perhaps a breakthrough in research on the whole peace movement. What that could be, none of us could imagine. But all of us were at this announced meeting.

"Friends," said the chairperson. "We have a unique opportunity. The time machine has now been perfected. Now we will be able to talk with persons who lived in other ages. We decided that the most worthy first use of this innovative technology would be the peace movement. And so today, each of you will have the chance to talk with some person in history who can help you in our search for an understanding of peace. Here are the ground rules: Your names will be drawn at random. When your name is drawn, you must say what peace leader in history you wish to interview. There will be no duplications. If someone has chosen the person you wish to interview, you must have an alternate choice. You will have fifteen minutes with that person. There will be no exceptions to these rules. Are there any questions? Good. Think about your choices. We will gather in twenty minutes to begin."

Frantically, my head spun as I sought that quiet within myself where wisdom might tell me whom I should request for my interview. Martin Luther King? Gandhi? Tolstoy? Woodrow Wilson? St. Francis? No, if my name was called late all those would be taken. What quiet, little noticed, but significant person of peace should I choose? Then, a thought came to my mind, and with it, comfort at my choice. I smiled, relaxed, and waited my turn.

When the meeting reconvened, names of journalists were drawn and they quickly made their choices. I was right. Everyone I had previously thought of had been chosen. My name was drawn twelfth of the fifteen, and I called out, "I wish to interview Mary of Nazareth." There were gasps, stares, and snickers at my choice. I had taken the risk. Either my interview would be a complete waste, or it might be a revolutionary breakthrough. I could only wait and see.

Before I really had time to collect my thoughts, I was being ushered down to the time machine booth. I tried to formulate the interview questions in my mind. What would I ask this woman? I guess I'd try to discover her role in the growth and development of the one called "Prince of Peace." But how to get at that? At that point, with my plan no more clearly formulated, the air was charged. There was some crackling, a few sparks from the dials in the booth, and there she was—a quiet, solid, rather plain elderly woman, the marks of hard, heavy work clearly showing in her hands and face. The digital clock on the wall started counting down from fifteen minutes.

And I froze. I tried just talking—every journalist has the gift of gab—but no words came to my tongue.

"Mary," I stammered, "I'm Jeff Norton from Peace

Press International in the twentieth century, and I am so pleased to meet you." Silence. No response. I panicked and started saying all those things I never thought I'd say. "If you only knew how many artists have painted you over the years, how many hospitals and churches are named after you." Again silence. Even though I had been assured that the equipment would translate my English and her Aramaic perfectly, it became clear that it did not translate centuries and cultures. I would need to get into her world. I glanced at the clock. Two precious minutes wasted already.

"Mary," I tried again, "I'd like to know about your contributions to the cause of peace."

"Peace? Shalom?" she spoke for the first time, gesturing vaguely as though I had asked her about the universe. I knew my questions had to become more specific, more concrete. Desperately, I rattled on, "I'll bet it wasn't easy to be the mother of Jesus."

"Easy, I should say not!" At last I had touched a common subject, and she enthusiastically and rapidly began to speak. "Once when his fame was rising, he came to Nazareth and spoke in the synagogue. First people loved him, and then they became so angry they almost threw him over the cliff. Said they would if he ever came back."

"What did you do?" I asked.

"Do? I took him home and gave him dinner. I don't care what *they* said. There was always welcome and peace for him in his home."

She continued, "And then there was the time when such huge crowds were coming to see him. My other children and I wanted to go see him. Bring him some good home cooked food. Enjoy the excitement a little. When we got there, someone told him, 'Your mother and brother and sisters are here to see you.' He did the

27

strangest thing; he turned to the crowd and asked, 'Who are my mother and brothers and sisters?' And then he told those strangers, 'You are my mother and brothers and sisters. Whoever does what God wants one to do is my brother, my sister, my mother.'"

"And then what happened?" I asked.

"I had to settle my other children down. Their feelings were really hurt; mine too, I guess. But I told them the best thing we could do for Jesus was to leave without a fuss. We would not embarrass him by pushing for time with him. When he was able, he would come to us. I did go back a little later, though. By then some nasty stories were going on about him. People said he was beside himself, maybe a little crazy. I knew how hard it was for him. I was afraid maybe it was too much. And so I went to see. We spoke only a few words. But I knew he was OK. It was the world that was mad. I went home and prayed for him."

"Mary, were you in Jerusalem the last week of Jesus' life?" She nodded. "Wasn't it dangerous?"

"Not for me—who's interested in an old woman?"

"Why were you there?"

"Because I thought he would need me. When I had brought him to Jerusalem to dedicate him as a baby years before, the aged Simeon had told me that a sword would pierce through my soul because of him. I felt that day was coming. And I would be there when he needed me."

I quietly responded, "You were right."

Her eyes glistened as she relived that fateful day. "I couldn't know why God allowed it to happen to the special one God sent through me. But at least my son knew I was there and that I loved him. With all the hatred, all the cruelty, we formed a little circle of love and peace. He spoke to me. And I think he died more quickly and easily after that."

"At that awful moment did you know that God would loose him again in the world?" I asked.

"I trusted God to accomplish God's purposes," Mary simply responded. "And so I stayed in Jerusalem awhile to pray and be with my son's followers. When I was no longer needed, I went home."

I wanted to linger on those memories, but the clock on the wall urged me on. I continued, "Mary, I believe your son was the one of whom the prophet Isaiah spoke—the Prince of Peace." She smiled enthusiastically at this. "I wonder, as his mother, did you help prepare him to be the Prince of Peace for all the world?"

She thought for a long time; I don't think she had thought about this before. Then she spoke very slowly.

"Well, I raised him to be a good boy. I didn't spoil him just because he was a special child. He knew how to obey. I really scolded him that time in Jerusalem when he was twelve and we lost him. I knew he'd have to go his own way soon, but he just wasn't raised that way. I taught him well."

"Anything else?" I queried.

"Yes, we tried to be a family of peace. There was so much hatred, so much fighting, so many people living close together but hating each other: Jews and Samaritans, Romans (of course), Syrians, and Phoenicians. We were at peace with ourselves and with God. We never spoke badly of any group of people. We respected all people."

"Anything else?" I pushed, sensing increasingly that this outspoken little peasant woman had ever so much to tell me. She paused for a moment to find those next words. "I knew God had purposes for my son. I knew that God would accomplish those purposes, at some time, in some way, even though I could not see the way. I just tried not to get in God's way. I did not want to hinder what God would do through my son."

I commented, "You were there for him. You supported him. You knew his needs."

She smiled at this bit of praise and acknowledged it. "I hope so," she said, "I think so."

The clock was racing relentlessly, and so I fired off my last question, "Mary," I said, "You had a very hard road with the Prince of Peace. There was so much loss, pain, and fear that you had to face. What kept you going?" And then I started to answer my own question, though as a journalist I knew better. "I suppose you got your inspiration when the angel came and spoke to you of the coming birth?"

"Ha! There was little comfort in that visit. I never wanted such a task. But then I figured that God did not often send a messenger to anyone, especially a woman. I chose to do what I was asked."

"Then perhaps the special visitors at the time of your son's birth gave you the strength for the life ahead."

"No. I wasn't surprised that visitors came. I thought God's messengers would want to share the news. But the moment that gave me strength came long before that. Do you want to hear about it?"

"Of course."

"Shortly after I learned that I would bear a child, I left Nazareth for a while. I was so hurt by Joseph's bitterness, the whispers, the looks. I had believed I was serving God, but then I felt so strange, so dirty. And so I visited my elderly kinswoman Elizabeth, who was also expecting a first child, also a wondrous birth. When we saw each other, it was so wonderful! We could tell our secrets. We could feel all right. More than that, we were caught up in God's mighty acts. That loving friendship with Elizabeth is something I will always remember. It was God's gift to me. So much so, that one day when I was with her I felt the Spirit of God filling me with song. I sang a hymn I'd never heard before. Elizabeth said it was something like the song of the great Hannah when she presented her son

Samuel. But it was God's mighty spirit moving these dull lips. I knew right then, that the God who did that could see me through all that I would face with the child."

"Do you remember the song, Mary?" I asked. "Would you sing it for me?"

The old voice grew strong and confident and rang out with a power from beyond herself as she sang,

My soul magnifies the Lord
  and my spirit rejoices in God my Savior,
for he has regarded the low estate of his handmaiden.
For behold, henceforth all generations will call me blessed;
  for he who is mighty has done great things for me,
  and holy is his name.
And his mercy is on those who fear him
  from generation to generation.

The clock gave the one-minute warning. Mary, however did not notice as she continued,

He has shown strength with his arm,
  he has scattered the proud in the imagination of their hearts,
he has put down the mighty from their thrones,
  and exalted those of low degree.

The clock clicked down to zero. I did not want this to end. I reached out to her, desperately hoping to keep her with me a few more moments. She grasped my hands for a moment and whispered, "Shalom, my son," and then her voice rang out again.

He has filled the hungry with good things,
  and the rich he has sent empty away.
He has helped his servant Israel, in remembrance of his mercy,
  as he spoke to our fathers,
to Abraham and to his posterity forever.

And she was gone.

The technicians kindly allowed me to remain in the booth a few minutes before they prepared it for the next interview. I sat wondering what I would tell my fellow journalists, for I had experienced more than I had learned. And yet, I suspected that rich learnings would emerge in time. If God had used the simple folk of Palestine twenty centuries ago on a mission of peace, was it not possible today in El Salvador and Nicaragua and Colorado? It occurred to me, that perhaps it was no coincidence that I had been granted this interview on Christmas Eve.

As I left the building to go out into the cold night air, was it my imagination that my tired old body didn't ache quite so much, that my cynicism didn't seem quite so hopeless? Could it really be true that though this peace campaign might take lifetimes, we were going to stick with it until everybody won? As I scraped the snow off my car, perhaps it was just the humming of the power line above me, but I think I really heard voices saying "Glory to God in the highest, and on earth, peace, good will to all."

THE PRACTICAL DREAMER

At first view, there was nothing striking about this man. His simple, well-worn clothes revealed him to be a man of small means. He was a person of few words, much more apt to show his feelings by arriving at your door with his tool chest to fix that stool, table, or door latch. This man was a doer, not a talker; he was an unassuming person, who stood patiently in lines, waiting his turn. If you know his family history well, you realize that royal blood flowed in his veins. He was a great-grandson (many generations removed), of the majestic King David. But he'd never tell anyone that, and seemingly it had little to do with his present life. No royal leisure for him. Indeed, a hard-working, hand-to-mouth existence was what he knew. He was a practical man, a craftsman; and yet he was a devout, considerate, and sensitive person. His loyalties and love, though seldom spoken, ran deep. Perhaps you have guessed that I am describing Joseph of Nazareth.

Have you ever seen a Christmas play where Joseph had the lead? Have you ever heard sermons or eulogies in praise of him? When examining a Nativity scene, once seeing Joseph present—did you ever pay him any attention? I'll wager your answers are no; if so, you are accurately reflecting the scriptural view of Joseph. For though he is mentioned, there is not recorded one single word that he spoke. His appearance is so brief that Joseph is mentioned only in the first two chapters of Matthew and of Luke. He has a walk-on, non-speaking part for one brief scene. Then he disappears from the gospel stage—forever. And yet so marvelous is this Christmas event, that there are fascinating stories surrounding the persons with bit parts. It is such a story that we now explore.

The scene is the small village of Nazareth. Most considered it a rather nondescript community in central Galilee. However, for at least two persons, it was a lovely and exciting place to be. Two families had completed their delicate negotiations through the matchmaker. They had agreed to a formal betrothal between Mary and Joseph. In the customs of the day, we might imagine quite accurately that Mary was in her early teens and that Joseph was perhaps ten years older. We may be quite sure that though they knew each other in this small village as acquaintances and friends, it was a family decision, not a personal decision, that led to their betrothal.

In order for betrothal to take place, the couple had to meet each other and give their consent. Once they gave consent, the formal betrothal period—usually lasting a year—began. They were absolutely bound to one another; though they could not live together, they were known as husband and wife. This betrothal could be broken only by death or by divorce.

Once the betrothal was sealed, Mary and Joseph discovered an excitement about seeing each other, thinking about the life they would share together in a year. We can imagine Joseph inventing carpentry errands that took him by Mary's house. We can picture Mary making a wide detour with her water jar on the way to the well and walking ever so slowly past Joseph's shop. Sometimes they were able to stop and visit for a few moments together at the door of the shop. Occasionally there was only the opportunity for a long glance at each other, as they looked into each other's soul and anticipated that day when they would share their lives with each other.

Just when they had reached that beautiful blend of excitement about each other and comfortableness with each other, something happened. With an air of gravity and urgency, Mary stopped by Joseph's shop one day. Usually she spoke to him briefly at the door and hurried on, fearful of gossip and rumors. This day she seemed so overwhelmed by something that such stories seemed of trivial concern. Mary first told him that she would be gone for a time to visit her kinswoman Elizabeth. Then she told him the most incredible tale. She said she had been picked by God for a unique purpose, that she was with child, but that this was not because of any wrongdoing on her part.

Quiet Joseph grew dark with hurt and anger, turned from her, clenched his fists, and skinned his knuckles as he pounded his bench. Mary dissolved into tears, running from his shop. As she left, she blurted out that she had hoped that at least *he* would understand. And she was gone.

Joseph was left alone. The loneliness was so much worse than before he had known Mary. There was an emptiness and a pain about his loneliness, a feeling of betrayal and loss. The haunting thought flitted across his mind that if lovely, innocent Mary could not be trusted, there must not be a person in all the world worthy of trust. Bitterly, he tried to fill his days with work. But his labors soon grew aimless. The usually efficient and frugal Joseph discovered himself absent-mindedly planing a whole board into shavings.

If the days were bad, the nights were worse. He tossed and moaned, sleeplessly pondering what he ought to do about Mary's strange news. It seemed he had only three choices: he could publicly accuse her of adultery—and she would be, at least, shamed, and maybe stoned; or he could marry her quickly and hope people did not count the months; or he could divorce her quietly without mentioning the grounds for divorce. He did not want to hurt Mary any more. At the same time, he could not feel his marriage was within the law and will of God if he married an adulteress. His tortured conclusion was that he would give her a quiet divorce in the presence of the minimum two witnesses required by law.

One fateful night he tossed and turned on his pallet on the floor of his shop. Never had his bed seemed lumpier or the floor harder. His plan for divorce seemed so logical, so right; why did he feel no peace about it? The next thing he knew, bright sunlight was streaming in his room. Surprisingly, he had slept for hours, and he felt at peace and happy. Why the difference? he asked himself. Then, dimly at first, he recalled a dream. The more he pondered, the more vividly he recalled that dream. An angel of the Lord had spoken to him through the dream. Now in the light of day the words of that angel of the dream were clearly ringing in his mind, "Joseph, son of David, do not fear to take Mary your wife, for that which is conceived in her is of the Holy Spirit; she will bear a son, and you shall call his name Jesus, for he will save his people from their sins."

Quite awake and sure, he bolted from his shop and ran all the way to Mary's house. Little did he know that just the night before, Mary had returned from Elizabeth's. He banged on the door with an enthusiasm that startled her family. When her father answered and opened the door, Joseph's and Mary's eyes met. In that moment she knew that they now both shared the secret. They would never need to speak of it to each other again. "Joseph, what do you want, so early in the morning?" her father asked. Breathlessly, Joseph explained that he would like to proceed with the wedding at once.

And so probably not more than a week or two later, after a modest wedding and marriage feast, Joseph took Mary to his rustic home in the back of the shop. But as the Matthew story tells us, he "knew her not until she had borne a son."

The first few months were sheer delight as they lived in the light of their visions. How lovely it was at the end of the day to smell the food cooking and hear Mary's singing. How peaceful were the evenings as they sat close together, she sewing infant's clothing, he rubbing down boards from which he would make a cradle. They had to be smooth—no splinters for Mary's child.

Then, frightening news jolted them out of their blissful existence. It was announced that persons must go to the province of their lineage to be enrolled for more of Caesar's taxes—and Mary was in advanced pregnancy. At first such a journey seemed impossible. Then the rightness that God's promised one be born in Bethlehem dawned upon them. And so resourceful Joseph bartered a lovely chest he had just made, which he had intended for his own home, for a beast of burden, a donkey. He carved a saddle and cushioned it with the softest cloth he could find. With exquisite care, he prepared to make this eighty-mile journey as comfortable as possible for his Mary.

Even with Joseph's careful planning, the trip was longer, more difficult, and more painful than they had anticipated. Just as the lights of Bethlehem came into view, Mary went into labor. How frantically he begged for a good room for her. How he inwardly cursed himself for not leaving her at home with her family and trusted midwife. How miserably he wished for a few extra gold talents in his money purse to buy his way past haughty innkeepers. But having no money, no friends, and no security, instead he used his resourcefulness to make her comfortable in an animal's stall and to be for her all that she needed, till—the pain ended, the exhaustion over— she brought forth her firstborn son and laid him in a manger.

Then came the delight, the wondrous delight, when awestruck visitors came to their makeshift, temporary little home, saying angels had informed them of the birth of this child. While Joseph was surprised, he was also deeply pleased. The message of other angels in the night to these visitors confirmed the message that the angel in his dreams had given him. His message had been no delusion. It was more real than life itself!

Some days later, after Joseph had found slightly more comfortable quarters for Mary and the child, more visitors arrived. These mysterious visitors, who came from distant lands, fell down, worshiped, and brought lavish gifts to the child. They explained that they had seen a marvelous new constellation, which, in its rising, portrayed a wondrous birth. They further explained that though King Herod had been confused and fascinated by their search, the scribes had been helpful. And finally all the pieces fell together for them as they gathered to pay homage to this child. With gracious farewells and deep bows, they backed from the room and were gone.

That evening as Joseph lay down to sleep, his inner feelings were a puzzle to him. Such beautiful things had happened to them; why did he feel uneasy, so restless? Surely his uncertainty was over; why could he not relax and enjoy the marvelous events that each new day with Mary and the child brought? Still puzzled, he dozed fitfully. And in his restless sleep, the dream angel spoke to him again. "Rise, take the child and his mother, and flee to Egypt, and remain there till I tell you; for Herod is about to search for the child to destroy him."

Joseph bolted into an upright position in bed. He looked

about him in fear. As the message of the dream drifted into his waking consciousness, he asked himself, was that just a bad dream, or is the Almighty guiding us? It didn't take him long to decide. Quietly he awoke Mary; together they quickly packed their belongings, including the expensive gifts just given them. Joseph loaded the donkey, put Mary upon it, and lifted the sleeping child into her arms. Immediately they set out on the highway south toward Hebron and beyond. It was a long, ambitious journey to Egypt—twice the length of their journey from Nazareth. The threats and dangers—ever unseen—seemed all around them. How do you look unhurried when you are in such a hurry to escape? How do you look inconspicuous when you feel that wife and child just glow with the divine promise, and therefore threaten a reigning king? For ten tortuous days—twenty miles a day—they journeyed, till at last they crossed the border out of Herod's jurisdiction. Only then were they safe. Joseph's skills meant he could find some work in this little Jewish settlement in Egypt. The sale of their precious gifts gave enough additional income so that there was food and shelter for this young homeless family. Then the news of a senseless slaughter of children in Bethlehem by order of a senile, insane king drifted down to them. Joseph and Mary were moved to speak prayers of compassion for the poor people of that village and prayers of gratitude to the Almighty in whose care they walked for a purpose.

Just a few months later Joseph's familiar dream angel again spoke to him at night. "Rise, take the child and his mother, and go to the land of Israel, for those who sought the child's life are dead." And so he did. When entering the province of Judea, they began hearing lurid tales of the cruelty of Herod's son Archelaus who was reigning in his father's stead. Uneasily they pondered; should they settle in Bethlehem or return to the province of Galilee where a milder son of Herod, Antipas by name, was tetrarch? For the fourth and final time the dream angel whispered, "Nazareth."

And so it was that they settled there. Mary and Joseph begot several children. The boy Jesus grew and matured. We catch only one more glimpse of Joseph. When Jesus was twelve, they went to Jerusalem for the Passover feast, as they devoutly did each year, and they almost lost the young man. At the conclusion of that story we see Joseph in character, concerned but not speaking.

Then he vanishes from the pages of history. Scholars guess that sometime between Jesus' twelfth birthday and his adult ministry at age thirty, Joseph died. That is not certain. All we know is that we do not hear from him again.

Yet, his influence lives on in the teachings of Jesus. Jesus often spoke of family life. Somehow, Jesus knew that fathers know how to give good gifts to their children. Somehow, he knew that the kingdom is like a father lovingly waiting for his runaway son, then lavishly welcoming and forgiving him. He said that when we pray, we should say "Our Father." In all this he was doubtlessly remembering this strong and capable, gentle and devout man who served as foster father to him.

Joseph, good-bye and thank-you. You have taught us it's OK to play a minor part in the drama of God's action in the world. No, that's not quite right. You have taught us something more: that in the service of Jesus the Christ, there are no minor parts. We thank you. Amen.

THE MISFIT

It was an age without hope in a world grown old. It seemed there was nothing sure in which to believe. Human genius had failed and confidence in human achievement had sunk with it. I found no grounds for a sure and certain confidence.

Oh, there had been a time when many had hoped the great Roman Empire would bring in a golden age of justice and prosperity. This had proved a fruitless hope. Their leaders engaged in the same petty competition. Roman rulers assassinated each other as freely as other kings. They expended much more men and money gaining their crown than using their crown for the people they ruled. It was good to have fairly reliable law and order—most of the time—but it was no cause to inspire faith and service.

Nor had the great philosophers and scholars given us a vision. We all longed for an ideal that would tell us how to live our lives. But the most popular philosophy of my day said simply "Eat, drink, and be merry, for tomorrow we die." I could not accept that, for I felt there must be more to life; but what?

I had turned to the study of the religions of humankind, hoping for a way to guide my life. But this pursuit disappointed me as well. Oh, I discovered many wise sayings and much beauty as I read the writings of ancient religions. But I also found much that appalled me, for I read of gods who were much less moral than I, doing all kinds of mischief on earth. And I read of so many gods, each different from one another. I knew that not all that I read could be true. But I had no way of sorting the true from the false. How I wished that the true God would speak with a clear voice, once and for all.

It was to the stars that I next directed my attention, for some saw the promise that the answer to human problems lay in those celestial bodies.

However, it wasn't so for me. The beauty and order of the stars in the heavens impressed me. I longed for a similar beauty and order on earth. But I found no direction from the stars for my life or for the world.

My many studies caused some people to hold me in awe. They called me "Magus," or "wise man." Folks looked to me for answers to the questions that haunt us all. It was an empty honor. Well did I know how little of my knowledge really mattered. Even better did I know that I had not found the answers for which I so earnestly sought. Increasingly the words of an ancient Jewish sage spoke what I felt, "Vanity of vanities, all is vanity. There is nothing new under the sun."

In my time, many tried to escape the meaninglessness of their existence by ever wilder orgies with ever new forms of depravity. I don't think it ever solved anything. Maybe it did help them forget for a few nights how short life is and how meaningless are those brief days.

I concluded that either there was no meaning to it all, or else God was yet to speak his most decisive message. How I longed that the latter be true.

If you understand how meaningless my life and how desperate my search, then perhaps you will understand my awed excitement that night. In my routine studies of the heavens, there appeared in an unexpected place a star of unusual brightness. I spent most of the night entranced by its beauty and wondering about its meaning. The next day when I awoke after my exciting observations, I asked myself, did I really see it or was it a dream, the product of my own desires? And so I called together a group of my colleagues to watch for it the next night. And yes, it did indeed rise again, even brighter and more mysterious than the night before.

Immediately we fell to discussing what it meant. Some said it was only a natural phenomenon, and that there must be some explanation. Some said it was a comet that would soon disappear. Others said it might be simply a conjunction of Saturn and Jupiter. Others suggested perhaps it was only Sirius the Dog Star, more clearly visible than before.

A few of us felt that it was the portent of some wondrous event. The God of the heavens was speaking to us. But what was this God saying? For once, all of that learning I had stored in my head was some good to me. I recalled a Jewish prophecy I had once read: "A star shall rise out of Jacob." Out of Jacob—a Jewish star—a leader, perhaps for the whole world this time, not just for one nation? Could our brilliant friend, the star, speak of that? We could only hope.

But how would we find out the message of the star? Some of us would have to care enough to go see. That would mean giving up all security, our possessions, and maybe even our lives. As we talked throughout the night it became clear to me. I had no choice. If this star was a sign from God, I just had to know its meaning. Perhaps the answer would speak to the deep hunger of my life.

Only a few of my companions shared my enthusiasm, so together we sold our possessions, arranged our loans, and equipped ourselves for this strange journey of unknown length and destination. How impatiently I awaited the time when we could finally be on our way.

Well, *finally* the day—I should say night—came. It was a beautiful, clear night. Our star was clearly seen. Our caravan assembled, we mounted our horses and our camels, and began our journey toward the star!

The journey was demanding, but, for a time, not difficult. We did have to travel at night to watch for our star's beckoning. Our travel was slow, cautious, and punctuated by many stops as we argued. Were we on the right way? Were we in harmony with our guiding star?

A frightening—though later funny—event occurred when we came to that checkpoint where we had to pay our road tariff taxes. As we awaited our turn I wondered, how do you explain such a journey to a petty Roman official? I tried to answer his routine questions honestly. Destination: unknown; Purpose of journey: follow a star to a new message from God. I could tell that poor official did not know whether we were subversive or harmless dreamers or crazy. Honestly, we didn't know either. I placed an extra silver talent in his palm, and he waved us on our way.

As we journeyed for days and the star seemed ever distant, we wondered, how will we know when we get there? Could we know we were immediately beneath the star? If so, how? We decided that if this star was from God, the Almighty One would give us another sign; what it would be, we had no idea.

Since the star did seem to be leading us toward Judea, we decided to stop in Jerusalem, the capital, to inquire. We made our way through narrow, winding streets, past the beautiful, shining new temple, and on to Herod's well-armed, luxurious palace.

A guard admitted us to a minor official who eyed us with some curiosity, and then asked us what we were seeking. I blurted out, "Where is he who has been born king of the Jews? For we have seen his star in its rising and have come to pay him homage."

It is impossible to adequately describe the impact of my words. A look of stark terror came across that official's face. A snap of his fingers, and we were surrounded by soldiers, their spears hemming us in. The official quickly disappeared into the inner chambers, and before we knew it, we were ushered into the presence of the fabled King Herod the Great, himself! The soldiers retreated to the edges, but kept alert and wary eyes on us.

My first impression of King Herod was one of disappointment. I had heard of his mighty and effective but ruthless rule for many years. What I saw before me was an old, physically weak man. He seemed to belong in bed to be cared for and to die a quiet death, rather than presiding over a wild, rebellious kingdom. His skin was an unhealthy yellow, his hand shook, and he could hardly stand. But there was still power in his voice when he spoke.

He wasted no time with introductions. Instead he roared, "What's this I hear about a new king? Some Maccabean pretender making trouble again?" We assured him we knew nothing of that. Still perturbed, he screamed "Then is there some guerrilla band fomenting rebellion up in the Galilean hills?" Again we answered that we knew nothing. "Then what's this rumor you bring of a new king?" he angrily asked. We quickly told our story of a star that seemed to herald a new event and that we thought perhaps it was from his kingdom that his earthshaking happiness would occur. Only slightly calmed, he told us "I will have my scholars investigate it for you. Meanwhile, you are not to leave. You *will* remain at the palace as my guests."

A nervous, frightened little man was assigned to us as our servant, and I presume, guard. We were given spacious quarters and rich food, but we were never left alone. I asked our nervous host why we seemed to frighten everyone so much. "Don't you know about Herod? A great man, a great king, but so suspicious," he whispered. "He's murdered his favorite wife Miriamne, his mother-in-law, and two sons, Alexander and Aristo-bulus. Another son, Antipater, is in prison right now. I fear your inquiry will cause another bloodbath—and you and I may be in it!"

Strangely, I did not feel fear, but I was frustrated. I was searching for something, but all that I had found so far was more jealously, suspicion, and intrigue. The air felt heavy and sick. Had the star deceived me? Had I deceived myself? At night I would step out into my little courtyard and look up. But the sky was overcast and I could not see my star. I could only wait.

In time we were summoned by Herod. A scribe with a scroll stood by his side. At Herod's nod, the scribe read, "From the prophet Micah:

And thou Bethlehem, land of Judah
Art in no wise least among the princes of Judah
For out of thee shall come forth a governor,
Which shall be a shepherd to my people Israel."

He dismissed the scribe and then said mockingly, in a voice full of irony, "Well, stargazers, there you have it, from a dusty old scroll in a back room of the Temple. I don't put much stock in such things—but investigate it if you wish. And when you find this wonderful child, tell me that I may pay him homage also."

That night we slipped out of Jerusalem. I'm sure Herod intended to have us shadowed, but the Almighty delivered us. We looked up. The sky was clear and our star was in the heavens. Once more we were in harmony with the star.

It is only five miles from Jerusalem to Bethlehem, traveling south. As we neared our destination, we were struck by the contrasts in the two cities: a small village of perhaps three hundred, rather than a huge metropolitan city of thousands. Here there were simple rural people, rather than power, suspicion, and intrigue. The contrast was greater than we had imagined. In this town, people knew of a wondrous child.

They guided us to a simple, earthen-floor home. The man had rented it as a temporary home for his wife and newborn son, who had been born in a manger. We found it without difficulty and were welcomed by the young family.

Without any external signs, I knew—this was the next sign for which we were seeking. Just as I knew that a star in the heavens spoke of an event on earth, so did I know that this family, this child on earth, came from purposes in the heavens. There was no extravagance here, only the simplest provision for life. Neither was there jealousy, suspicion, or murder. Rather, there was love, trust, peace, joy, and hope! The contentment in that woman's eyes as she rocked her child! The compassion of that man as he hovered about her, clumsily helping with the child! Their total lack of surprise that Magi from hundreds of miles away should be guided to this child. The mystery of our star was solved. Yet more mystery remained—the mystery of all that God would accomplish through this wondrous child.

We felt such joy and relief when we found this child. We laughed and cried at the same time. We fell on our knees, nay, on our faces in adoration before him. We ran out to our packs, and with joyful abandon, threw open our chests and drew from them our remaining treasures. They seemed much too small for such a child as this. At the same time, these gifts must have seemed lavish to his needy parents—our gold, frankincense, and myrrh.

It must have been nearly dawn when, with a sense of satisfied completeness, we told them good night and left to have a good sleep. However, our sleep was short and fitful. I had a dream of Herod with a sword poised over the child. And then the message, "Do not return to Herod."

We quickly packed and prepared to go another way. Though we stopped to warn the young family, Joseph too had been guided in dream, and they were packing to escape to Egypt. We bid a hasty good-bye and began a swift journey to the north, a journey we did not stop till we were safely beyond Herod's borders.

Now that my journey is over, I wonder, why do I now view my world so differently? What happened to me? I can only answer that God granted me a discovery that has turned my world right side up: God has chosen what the world calls foolish to shame the wise; he has chosen what the world calls weak to shame the strong. He has chosen things of little strength and small repute. I now look for God everywhere. I believe that things will turn out all right and there will be wonderful surprises. You might say I have been reborn. I have looked into the face of a wonder child. And now I have hope.

MESSAGE FROM THE MANGER

My problem is that I always want to know more than they tell me! I mean, I open my Bible and read such brief, cryptic stories. I'm curious about what else happened! This was especially true as once more I read those tantalizingly brief stories in Matthew and Luke about Jesus' birth. You see, I had been working on an important theological question, and those stories seemingly shed no light at all. The theological question I was exploring was this: If God was uniquely present and at work in Jesus, when did God begin to work through him? Was it after his baptism as a grown man, or when he began his ministry some time later? Did it start with his childhood, his birth, or his conception?

I seemed to have come to a dead end on my investigation at every point. There simply was no evidence on which to base a judgment. And then, a thought came to mind. Once in a while, in the depths of my imagination, I had succeeded in summoning a first century Middle Eastern detective: Azad the Stealth was his name. He had uncovered some most interesting information for me in the past. For a time I resisted using Azad, since he held little interest in my theological pursuits. But then, since I had no one else to help me, I summoned him. And there he was, wearing his usual grubby clothes and mischievous smile. He didn't seem at all surprised to see me; I suspect he had been getting my vibes and was expecting my call.

After our usual embrace and drink together, I told him of my assignment for him. I tried to put it in terms he could understand. I simply said I wanted to know how people responded to the birth of this child, Jesus. He couldn't believe I'd pay money for that, but he shrugged his shoulders and said, "OK, if that's what you want." I told him the few details known from the Bible accounts and asked him to give me as much direct dialogue with people as possible.

He reminded me that this investigation would include a lot of travel and be very costly. I knew he was building up for the haggle on price. We would both be disappointed to miss that. I hid from him how desperately I wanted this information, and he probably hid from me how badly he needed the work. Eventually, we agreed on a travel allowance and a basic fee, though we both knew that I would reward him further if the reports were unusually helpful. I urged promptness on this assignment, and he said he would set to it at once. I bid him good-bye and waited eagerly. The first communiqué was labeled thus:

From: Azad

Location: Bethlehem

Subject: Women at the manger

(Goodness, I thought, he's never reported this formally before. Did he stick around and take a writing course?)

Report of Interview: As you suggested, Dick, I first contacted Miriam, the innkeeper's wife. Following is our conservation:

I told her that I represented a friend of Joseph and Mary who would like to locate them and know more about them.

"I have no idea where they went," Miriam said. "But I can tell you about them when they were here."

"I understand you provided the only available place for them," I said. "And that was the one kind act in the whole trip."

"Oh, anyone would have done it," she said. "Such beautiful people and so frightened. But you are wrong. Many people were kind to them."

"Oh? Can you give me names and addresses?"

She laughed. "That's hardly necessary. It's mostly the women of the neighborhood. When they heard it, they all dropped by. Usually each had some needed item—blankets or clothes from their own children. Each found something to share. Food was scarce, but many a woman cooked something extra and brought it to the family. They wanted that baby to be taken care of."

"Very nice," I answered. "Anything else you can tell me?"

Miriam thought for a moment. "Only this," she quietly replied, "We've found each other again. When we ran into each other visiting the baby, we realized how long it had been since we'd spent time together like that. The fear of the soldiers, the harsh times—I don't know, but we had all pulled back into ourselves. Somehow we all rallied together around that young family. When they left suddenly, we promised each other not to let our rediscovered friendships die. And we haven't. I don't feel so alone anymore, and I am happy about that."

Not much here, but that's what you wanted. I'll keep looking.

The next communiqué came rather promptly after that.

From: Azad

Location: Bethlehem still. (This isn't much of a town. You should give me hardship pay for my time here.)

Subject: Shepherds. No one gave names. I think they are mostly fugitives from the law and thought me a Roman spy. This was not easy.

I asked, "Did angels come visit you?"

"Ask them!" somebody said. Another pitched in, "Maybe they did and maybe they didn't." Another asked, "Why do you want to know?" And still another a little more seriously responded, "Well, something happened. We don't quite know whether it was lightning, or a star falling out of the heavens, or what."

I asked, "Did you go see the baby?"

Again the answers were jumbled, "Yes, some of us did." "Naw, if you've seen one baby you've seen them all."

"Then what?" I asked.

One man fairly seriously replied, "Well, most of us just saw them and came back and pretty well forgot about it. But not old Zebech."

I asked, "What about Zebech?"

The same man responded, "You should ask him. No, he probably wouldn't talk. He's out with the sheep by himself now—I think he's spent too much time out there by himself with the sheep." (He tapped the temple of his head to signify what he thought of Zebech's mental status.) "He's a bachelor, an old man. But more than the rest of us, he was really taken with that baby. He tried to find some gift to take to the baby every day. Maybe he'd take a warm fleece. Or he'd make a shepherd's pipe. Or find a pretty stone. One day he came back from seeing them so excited and happy. I asked him what had happened. He said the mother had told him that he didn't have to bring a gift each day, that he was their friend and he was welcome any time."

I asked, "How did he take it when they left?"

And the same young man responded, "That's when he got really strange. He'll usually talk about that himself. Maybe you ought to go see him. It's that little pasture at the top of this rock incline."

And so I climbed up to see him. He *was* strange! He knew I was there but paid no attention, looking straight at the sheep. I spoke first, "I hear you liked the baby." He smiled, but still said nothing. "What did they look like—that family?" I asked.

"The baby had lots of dark hair."

"Were they tall or short?"

"And deep blue eyes."

"Were they fat or thin?"

"And a dimple on his right cheek. His mother said he smiled when he heard my voice."

"Did the father wear a beard? Did the mother?"

"The baby squeezed my fingers when I held them out."

"Can you describe the parents?"

"I don't know. I can't remember."

I persisted. "I'm a friend, and I need to know what happened that last day."

He fell silent for a bit. When he spoke, he seemed to be reliving that day. "I had watched through the night shift and thought to go take them a little fresh goat's milk for their breakfast. When I got there, they were hurriedly packing. Joseph said he had a dream that Herod would send soldiers to kill the child. I kissed the baby good-bye and then ran back to shepherd's field. I shouted at the others to help me move the flock and began stirring them together myself. I gave no explanations, but we had that narrow gorge filled with sheep when the Roman soldiers arrived. They shouted at me and caned me, telling me to get those sheep out of the way. I pretended not to understand and kept shouting at the others to keep the sheep swirling in their way, blocking the whole canyon. In time they got through, of course. I was sore from their blows for weeks. And it took us days to round up the sheep. But it was worth it. The baby had two or three more hours head start on them. I hope he's still safe, wherever he is."

He became silent again and I left him without saying good-bye. You're paying me good money to find out that a strange old bachelor shepherd lost his head over the baby?
—Azad.

I was pleased with Azad's reports, though I must confess I didn't know any more what they were telling me than he did. I would have to wait for further reports to see if the puzzles would fit together—a wait that was longer than I anticipated. The next communiqué revealed why.

From: Azad
Location: Ecbatana, Regnum Parthicum (Persia to you)
Topic: Melchior, a Magus.

What a long, horrible journey to find this man. See attached bill for camel train and drivers. [*I gasped.*] See also bill for olive oil liniment to ease the pain of my bones after so many days' ride.

When I walked by the palace of this learned man, I knew I'd never gain admission looking like I did. See bill for new robe, a trip to the baths, and trimming of my hair and heard. [*I ran a quick total in my head and thought, Boy, Azad, this better be good!*]

After all this, I presented myself as a scholar who had traveled far to inquire of Melchior's greatest discovery. After a long wait, I was told that Melchior would see me on the morrow.

I was surprised by what I saw. Here was a distinguished, but frail, very old man. I wondered how he endured the same journey I had just taken.

His talk, however, was of stars and the messages that are in them. He spoke of the brilliant comet streaking across the skies speaking of some event that was then to be revealed. He spoke of the brilliant conjunction of Saturn and Jupiter. And then his voice lowered and he said, "But when on the first day of the Egyptian month Mesori (which means, "birth of a prince") Sirius the Dog Star rose heliacally and shown with extraordinary brilliance, I knew the day had come. I called my colleagues and we journeyed to that mysterious land where the new prince would be revealed to us." I hope you understand this; I don't. I wrote it down just as he said it. Well, I tried to nudge him along toward our subject; but he loved having a listener, and he talked on and on.

"How carefully we selected our gifts for the new king. Caspar would bring frankincense, Balthasar would bring myrrh. And I would bring lavish amounts of the costliest and most beautiful fabrics—linen and silk for his kingly robes." *[Wait, I thought. You journeyed all that way and spent all that money and can't even get it right, Azad? The report rambled on.]*

"And so we made our way in the general direction of the star at its rising. We travelled only those hours before dawn when we could see it most clearly, and then only on cloudless nights."

I urged him on again. "Tell me about the king you discovered."

"We expected mystery and adventure on this quest, but we did not know what direction it would take. When we got to Judah there was a frightful confusion. They knew nothing about the star or the prince. Their king was angry—I think he was often angry. The people were frightened; I must say I don't blame them. But they did dredge one clue out of their sacred writings, helping us to find him in Bethlehem."

Azad's report continued, "I asked for his impressions of the holy family."

Melchior responded, "Oh, very strange, very strange. We found them in an abandoned hut that was about to collapse." [Note from Azad: they moved from the stable to the hut for a few weeks.] "They apologized for their simple, temporary quarters, but no matter. We thought, so this is the Almighty's secret. The star in its rising speaks of a peasant king who will arise from among his people, a prince of peace. Surely the Majestic One who can speak through the Dog Star can act through this lovely infant from this peaceful family. We were filled with awe at their quiet majesty. We fell down and worshipped. Somehow as I looked at that smiling, peaceful infant, I knew. I knew that though my days are soon over, the Almighty's purpose will continue through the centuries, carried on by that child. I will not live to see his peaceable kingdom, nor will I know how he will bring it about. But I have no doubt that such a kingdom there will be."

There was a far-off shine in his eye as he said this—and a little bit of the tenderness I had seen in old Zebech. I asked him, "Did you give them the gifts?"

"Oh," said he, "I almost forgot. When I saw this infant king and his poor parents, suddenly our gifts did not seem right. This family looked like sparrows poised for flight. And there was so much danger and tension all around. My gift of bolts and bolts of fine material would be worse than useless to them. My companions went ahead and gave their gifts of frankincense and myrrh, but I changed my mind. I gave them all my gold—my treasure that I carried for travel expenses and emergencies. And they seemed grateful. I trust it bought their way through some of the terror that was all about them. I bartered the fine fabrics to buy my way back to Ecbatana."

That's all he told me. I now sign off to saddle my camel for the long ride back. Oh, I forgot to mention something. I tried to trace Joseph and Mary in their flight from Jerusalem. The border guard into Egypt would not let me by. All I could do was bribe him so I could look at his ledger. I discovered that Joseph, wife Mary, and child Jeshua were allowed to pass into Egypt (I wonder how much of a gold bribe *that* took) and then several months later returned. That's all I could find down there.

—Azad

I braced myself that with the distances and travel, it would be a long time before I heard from Azad, and it was.

I waited and reread his previous reports. Still I feared that at the end of all of Azad's efforts, I would have to conclude that we didn't know when God began to work in Jesus. But I waited and hoped.

Finally another communiqué arrived. I eagerly opened it, and this is what I read:

From: Azad

Location: Nazareth

Subject: Well, you'll see.

Your sources were correct. After disappearing for some time, they are now back in Nazareth. Joseph has reopened his shop and business seems good. Jeshua (or Jesus, as you say it) now has a little brother and a baby sister.

I did not think it wise to interrogate them directly, and so I have set up surveillance across the street. I discovered, however, that their neighbors are most eager to talk about them.

They say that neither Joseph nor Mary will say much about where they have been, why the tax trip took so long, or any other details. They seem to want not to call attention from the authorities to themselves. But they are good neighbors, as they always were. They say that both Joseph and Mary have changed. Joseph was always a good craftsman, but rather severe and businesslike. Now he is heard to whistle in his shop. On a rainy day he may be seen carving toys, not only for his own children, but for the children of the village. And children are welcome in his shop, can ask all the questions they want. They say that Joseph has become so soft and tender. He is a marvelous father to his children.

Mary has changed also, they say. She used to be so shy and withdrawn. No longer. She is talkative and outgoing. There is no doubt that she is the strongest influence on those children. There's a power, an authority about her. No one had better do harm to those children; they'd have one tough woman to deal with. Even more, they say Mary looks like she is bursting with some big secret that she cannot tell. Once in awhile she is heard to sing a song that she said the Almighty gave her some years before. The only phrase my informant could remember is this: "He who is mighty has done great things for me, and holy is his name."

As for me, I watch them. Some evenings at the end of the day Mary and Joseph relax and play with the children in their tiny yard. Sometimes they carry their evening meal to the hillsides outside town and let the children run and play in the meadows. As I watch them, I see beauty, love, and peace.

Jeshua is now a bright four-year-old. He particularly loves to be out-of-doors. He enjoys the flowers, but rarely picks them. He delights in the lilies of the field and the birds of the air, and indeed, seems to be at one with them. That's about all I can tell you.

Otherwise, I think I have now finished my project. If you have any other leads, let me know. I don't know if you have solved your problem, but I have done what you asked. Will you please send me the balance of my fee and expenses?

Your obedient servant, Azad.

Now I was on my own again. This had been Azad's finest, most sensitive work for me; but still I was puzzled. I tried to summarize all he had told me. Let's see. This baby—

—had been the magnet that drew Miriam and the Bethlehem women into close community with each other.

—had broken through the crust of a grizzled old bachelor shepherd, Zebech, and stirred him to unusual courage.

—had consoled the aged Melchior about his own death and gave him hope for God's purpose in future generations.

—had drawn out the gentle, tender side in Joseph, allowing him to be more human.

—had liberated Mary to be strong and more confident, allowing her to be more fully human.

And yet, I thought, any child anywhere could do those things. Were these simply human responses to a loveable manger baby, or was this God's beginning work in this person?

Only then did I discover that the answer had been before me all the time; but until Azad's discoveries, I had not eyes to see. In that Christmas story, the angel says all in these words "For to you is born *this day* in the city of David, a Savior, who is Christ the Lord." As that child came as a special gift of God, he drew loving, generous responses. And ever since that birth, we see God's continuing work through the birth of each child that has come into the world. There is much more to it than that, of course, but this is where the miracle begins.

With at least this one problem illuminated, I sent my thank-you note and final check to Azad. My generosity must have startled him so much that he didn't even know how to thank me. He responded, "I have received your payment. It is satisfactory, but I think that baby must have softened your brain as well. This is a most interesting case, and I shall observe it closely as often as possible, in case you have future questions. Until then, shalom. Your able and obedient and willing and humble servant, Azad the Stealth."

And Azad, for helping me hear the message from the manger, I salute you. Shalom and amen.

THE MEMORIES OF EBEN BEN ADAM

My name is Eben Ben Adam. This white hair and beard tell the truth about me. The Almighty has already granted me at least my three score years and ten. And though I tire very easily and walk slower, I trust that I will be granted a few more years to lead my clan and tend those flocks—I hope so.

I am a shepherd, as was my father, and my father's father. So is my son, as will be my son's sons.

Occasionally we journey up north to Bethlehem or even Jerusalem for a few days to sell our wool and animals. All of the rest of our time is spent with our flocks in these hills and valleys. I know not how many thousand days and nights I have faced weather of all kinds watching over these flocks. Nor do I know how many hundreds of times I have tramped over this very place in our endless search for food and water.

But do not misunderstand me. I complain not of monotony. How could anything be monotonous when each day I must look at the sun, the stars, and the clouds for signs to guide me? When each day I must watch the motion and listen to the sounds of the flock for either messages of contentment or of sickness or danger? When each day I must check the grass for poisonous plants, scout out a watering place, and plan my next movement? When any moment—day or night—might bring attack from an enemy, whether it be serpent or wild animal or thief? Though an old man, I am still alert, and the alertness has served me well. My kinfolk and servants are well-fed.

But what was I saying? Oh yes, when all is quiet and I have moments to sit and think, even then I am not bored. For in those moments, my mind wanders over my memories. Most of all, that one most glorious week of my whole life.

It was many years ago, a clear starlit, but very dark night. I was to take the second watch, so I was trying to get some sleep by the fire. Sleep did not come; restlessness troubled me. I had heard that wild rumor that a month before, some of my shepherd friends had heard and seen angels. I did not know whether to believe that or not. As I say, I was troubled and restless. I know not why. Then, I heard it—a sound so muffled that the dull of ear would not hear it—the sound of sheep becoming wary and moving about when they had already settled for the night. As I peered into the darkness to see what it might be, all of a sudden I heard a shout, "Stop, thief!" I jumped to my feet as Job, one of my hired hands, roughly pushed two people before me. Job hurriedly cried out that he had caught them. They had been walking feverishly, nearly running, through the night. They were some distance from the road. To us it seemed obvious that they were trying to steal some of our herd.

As the two drew to closer the campfire, I could see that it was a man and a woman. The woman was carrying a large bundle, which was presently revealed as a small child, just a few months of age. The man denied all of Job's charges and asked to talk to me privately.

I took him aside and asked, "Are you trying to steal my sheep?" He shook his head no. "Then are you running from something?" He responded, "I guess so." I asked, "Did you commit some crime?" Again he shook his head no. Still puzzled I asked, "Then why are you running?"

And he quietly responded, "Because God told me to. In a dream he told me to take the child and his mother and flee to Egypt."

I wanted to laugh in his face, and yet there was something that stopped me. There was a bit of mystery about this couple. They seemed so fearful and yet confident at the same time; so fatigued and weak, and yet so strong. Not knowing what to say, I said, "You may rest here for the night. We will protect you. There's probably still some remains from our supper over by the fire." He thanked me and quickly returned to his wife and child. Shortly after they had eaten and settled for the night, it was my turn to take the watch. I had a good long sleepless night to ponder things. In the shivering moments just before the dawn, I decided what I would do; though I did not then know why.

As my three hired hands, the man and his wife, and I were gathered early in the morning for some bread and warm goat's milk I told them, "Today, I am going to begin my drive south. If you and your wife would like to stay with us and help with the drive, you may. Joseph, you may help with the herds, and you, Mary, may help with the food. There will be a place among our sleeping robes where you may lay the baby. If there are ever outsiders in camp, you must keep him very quiet." I then went to our supplies and found some rather ragged shepherd's clothes for both of them. "You will attract less attention if you shed those townspeople's clothes and wear these," I told them.

No one said a word, but I could read the faces of my hired hands: shock, and then anger. Anger that I would risk my life and theirs and all our possessions to harbor fugitives from the law. I was their master, so they said not a word, but rather packed our belongings and made sullen preparations to drive our flocks to the south.

Though my men resisted me at first, they soon were caught up in the adventure of it all. There was a sense of excitement in our camp. Somehow, it is exhilarating to be a smuggler! Then too, all of us became rather quickly attached to the child. We hadn't quite realized how lonely we were and how nice it was to have a family among us. The men developed signals so that by their whistles, she knew whether she could carry her child or had to keep him out of sight. We all grew so casual about everything. It was as though we were all acting a part or playing a game. Once in a while we'd burst out laughing at our huge make-believe.

On the second day of our journey, my cousin Caleb came into camp riding his horse at a furious pace. "Do any of your men have their families with them?" he asked.

"Caleb, you know I'm a widower. Both Josh and Abe are still bachelors, and Job's wife stays in Hebron waiting to spend his pay."

"You can thank the Almighty for that," Caleb returned. "Herod's troops have just sacked Bethlehem, killing every baby boy two years old or under. Must have murdered twenty or thirty little fellows in cold blood. Those soldier swine! Who knows, they may be sweeping the countryside next."

"Thank you for the information kinsman," I told him, "but that has nothing to do with me." As he galloped out of camp, Mary looked very ill and shook with sobs. We men put our heads together trying to plan the best course. Should we push the flocks faster and get out of range, calling attention to ourselves? Or should we go at a more typical pace and hope to escape detection? We decided on the latter course and continued slowly to the south, toward the border of Egypt.

Early in the afternoon of the fifth day of our journey we heard Josh's frantic warning whistle. Just as Mary hurriedly put the child under cover and quieted him, a whole century of Roman soldiers galloped into our midst. Hoping I wasn't shaking too much, I ran up to the captain to see what they wanted. It was the same captain I had met in this region several times before. He asked what I was doing and why I was moving in the direction I was. I gave him a long answer about how the sheep needed a different kind of grass to be ready for the market. It was obvious he didn't know anything about sheep and wasn't interested. He waved me off before I finished. All the time I spoke, Mary was bent over our sleeping robes seeming to sew a pretended rip in one of the robes. She was absorbed in her work. I don't think any of the soldiers even realized she was not a lad. They certainly did not realize what a treasure she kept still beneath that top robe! It must have been a routine Roman patrol, for they left rather hurriedly without searching. As they went, they scooped up a couple of my fattest prize lambs. They said that the lambs would make a good supper—a token of my appreciation for Roman protection, they said. I protested a little, as they expected me to, but fell silent when the sergeant raised his hand with the whip in it. As they galloped over the hill, I could see Joshua's huge grin of relief from half a mile away!

Most of the rest of the time we traveled without incident. My favorite times of all were the evenings, when the day's work was over and the evening meal eaten.

Then, when all was quiet save for the friendly nighttime noises, Mary would sit by the campfire and play with her baby. I would watch them till the fire had died to red embers and it was long past my usual time for resting. I heard Josh and Abe laughing about it one night. "Looks like Eben has himself a girlfriend," they said. Usually I would have cracked their heads together for such a remark as that, but I did not care.

But they were all wrong; it was not for that reason that I stayed so close to them. Oh, I will admit, Mary did have the slightest resemblance to my beloved Rachel, my beautiful Rachel who had died trying to give birth to my first child scarcely more than a year after she became my bride. When we buried her with the stillborn child in her arms—it seemed that they had buried me, too. Though I moved and worked and ate, I would only go through the motions. I could not laugh or cry, and would not care for anyone or anything. I did not want to be so horribly hurt and lost again. Anger and bitterness were my only feelings. I think I died with her.

But as I sat at the campfire near that mother and child, I sensed that just maybe I could come alive again. I never saw anything so beautiful as the sheer love and joy that was shared by that mother and child. At one moment Mary would remind me of a newborn lamb. Have you ever looked into the eyes of a freshly born baby lamb, ever seen all the innocence and beauty and eagerness for life that is there? At times she looked like that. But at other times her eyes sparkled as if she had some great big job, some wonderful secret that, if she had to keep it inside any longer, she was just going to burst. Oh, I tell you even now I can shut my eyes and see that lovely, excited mother and child across the campfire from me.

I remember well that last evening we sat there. Sometimes Joseph sat with us, but this evening he was out helping with the watch. He tried to do his part, even though he was no shepherd. I had told Joseph that we would risk unwanted attention if we went any further, and there were no pastures to provide for our sheep. He had agreed that they would go on by themselves the next day.

And so I sat by the campfire, knowing it would be the last time I would ever gaze upon that beautiful mother and child. As that realization hit me, I found it painful to take every breath, and I scarcely trusted my voice to speak for me. How my arms ached to embrace her and thank her for the hope she and the child had brought to my life. However, it is not done so in our land. Our women present themselves with modesty and we treat them with dignity and respect. Instead, I asked if I might hold the child for a while, and she let me. I wanted to tell her all that these days had meant to me. Twice I tried to speak, but no words came. Finally I choked out, "Joseph is a very lucky man—to have such a loving wife and such a beautiful child."

Somehow those words touched Mary, and the secret burst from her as she nearly shouted to me. "Oh he's beautiful; but he's so much more. He's God's gift to the world. Through him God is going to set people free!" And then, on an impulse, she came to me. We hugged the baby while we both cried and sprinkled him with laughter, or laughed and sprinkled him with tears. I suppose Mary was relieved that there was now someone with whom she could share her secret. I trembled with emotion as I felt huge rocks of bitterness slipping away. The floods of grief washed through me, and fresh showers of relief fell upon me. When the sobs finally ended, I felt more relieved and more at peace than I ever had in my whole life. I slept more soundly than I had since my childhood and didn't awaken till the sun, high in the sky, hit me squarely in the face. Joseph and Mary were already up and ready to leave.

Though I had dreaded this moment, now I felt no sadness. Joseph gripped my hand long and told me that Yahweh had directed us together. Mary nodded and said ever so softly, "Thank you for all your kindness." They were on their way. Shortly they disappeared over a hill, and I have never seen them again.

I did not weep at our farewell because I then anticipated

what I now know: that they never really left me. Every day since, my life has been illuminated by that time we spent together.

Mark you well, I have changed—in so many ways. For one thing, I see so many lovely things that once I missed. Each time I see unexpected beauty, in a flower or an animal, or a sunset or a rainbow, I see the handprint of the Almighty. And I pause to give thanks. Then too, I enjoy my servants more. I used to think that kindness would spoil them. But there exists a real trust and respect between us now that makes my load ever so much easier. Then, I decided to risk loving and caring again. I married once more, and my wife, Becky, gave me first a daughter and then a son. My daughter is now a woman and recently gave birth to her firstborn son; they named him after me. My son has become my legs as I try to keep up with these flocks. He is keen and eager and soon will be able to manage the herds for me.

Yes, my life has truly changed and all because a child and his parents came and lived with me for a time. That was many years ago. He must be a man now. I don't know where he is or what he is doing. I only know that I have already experienced the deliverance his mother promised. For me the words of the ancient prophet have been fulfilled:

"For to us a child is born, to us a son is given. . . .
    And his name will be called
      Wonderful Counselor,
        Mighty God,
          Everlasting Father,
            Prince of Peace."

ROOT OUT OF
DRY GROUND

Who has believed what we have heard?
  And to whom has the arm of the Lord been revealed?
For he grew up before him like a young plant,
  And like a root out of dry ground.

Isaiah 53:1-2

So wrote the later Isaiah some five hundred years before the birth of Jesus. In that profound statement about the suffering servant of the Lord, a statement Jesus was to embrace as his very own, Isaiah included a striking phrase. He said the servant was "like a root out of dry ground." That is to say, that in rather unpromising, unfertile, dry soil, a plant took root. One might expect the plant to be stunted by the soil in which it was planted, but it was not so. Rather the roots ran deep and took hold. Though much a part of the soil, but different from the soil, that root out of dry ground flourished, flowered, died, sacrificed self for others, and resurrected—giving life to countless others.

Each year I tell a story that in some way explores the meaning of the Christmas event. Usually I have concentrated on one person. This is the story of the land, the dry ground out of which the root which is called Jesus Christ sprang. I have been privileged to visit this land twice as part of a continuing quest to understand the biblical faith better. I must say that when I arrived there, the area had a most familiar look. With the exception of my own country, there is no part of the world whose history and geography I have pursued more carefully or with greater interest and fascination.

Let me tell you some things about this land. Because of the many important events that have occurred there, some people visualize Palestine as a huge, powerful land. It is not. It is roughly the size and shape of Vermont, turned upside down. Of course, it is impossible to tell you the exact dimensions of this land, for like many other countries, its boundaries have changed many times, reflecting the power of the government ruling it and the power of its neighbors. It never exceeded an area 120 to 150 miles long and 30 to 50 miles wide. (Oh, to be sure, there were a few short years when the great kings David and Solomon tenuously held a kingdom about twice that size; but those years quickly ended, never to return).

We can concentrate on the smaller boundaries 120 miles north to south, 30 to 50 miles east to west. The variation in the width of this land comes from the sloping shoreline of the Mediterranean Sea, sometimes called the Great Sea, which forms its western boundary.

Palestine has been called a geographic marvel, the earth scientists' paradise, the land of infinite variety. Truly amazing geographical variations occur within this small area. It includes the lovely Sea of Galilee, which is almost seven hundred feet below sea level. The Jordan River channels the Sea of Galilee's fresh water and empties it into the salt-water basin known as the Dead Sea. The name *Jordan* means *descender*; an appropriate word, for in the sixty-five mile distance from Galilee to the Dead Sea, there is a six hundred-foot drop. The Dead Sea is fully one-fourth of a mile below sea level. It is the lowest place in the world—being about five times as far below sea level as Death Valley, California. In contrast is majestic Mount

Hermon in the north, towering 9,200 feet above sea level.

Palestine has four diverse bands of land running north and south. The land bordering the Mediterranean Sea is a flat and fertile coastal plain. Next to it rises the central hilly plateau. Jerusalem and Bethlehem are located within this plateau. A valley that contains the Jordan and the Dead Sea are located in the third section. And in the last band, the table lands of the Transjordan rise on the eastern side of Palestine.

Palestine lies between thirty-one and thirty-three degrees north latitude. This is the same parallel as Georgia, Arizona, Nagasaki, and Shanghai. However, because it is adjacent to the Mediterranean Sea, its weather is moderate with two seasons. There is a cool winter with some rain and occasionally, but not frequently, snow. In the summer, the sun shines most of the time.

At the same time, there is a wide variety in the forms and altitude of its terrain. It includes ranging mountains and deep Dead Sea depressions, valleys, and blazing deserts. Local climates in Palestine can vary from subarctic to torrid.

This land is of interest also because of its location. It is located on the bridge of land between three continents. Further, it was north of the Nile region where the great Egyptian empires would rise, and south of the Tigris and Euphrates rivers where many strong civilizations would rise. Palestine was the crossroads of the world, but it was harassed by the powerful empires on either side. Sometimes it would be drawn into intrigues and difficulties with both sets of empires.

This brings us to the most interesting part of the story about the land—the people who lived there. It seems that this land was wanted by many people. People after people occupied it. To live there, they had to conquer the people who lived there before. In this land you will find the ruins of city after city that was built on the same spot, only to be conquered and destroyed by the next group of people who wanted to occupy it. As Paul L. Maier, author of the book, *First Christmas* (Harper & Row, 1971), observed, "It may well have been [—and is—] the most bitterly contested spot on earth."

Eighteen centuries before the birth of Christ, a man named Abraham wandered through it, sensing that as part of the covenant with God, his descendants would claim this land. But he was only a tenant, a nomad. Centuries later, Abraham's descendants appeared on the border again, this time many in number, armed with a restored covenant with their God and a burning conviction that God would give them this land. They went up and claimed it, not without violence of their own, for this seemed to be the only way.

From these people rose three sturdy kings: Saul, David, and Solomon, who for a time rallied the people together, captured and founded a capital of Jerusalem, and made the country—for a century or less—a first-class military and political power.

When Solomon died, nine hundred years before Christ, there was a civil war and revolution. The northern tribes split, set up a separate government, and in a couple of centuries, they were captured, dispersed, destroyed, and never heard from again.

Once the Israelites were on this land, it seemed everyone wanted to take it from them. Through the centuries they endured invasions and attacks by the Assyrians, the Babylonians, the Egyptians, the Syrians, the Greeks, and finally the Romans. More than once Jerusalem was captured and burned, her choicest people exiled to lands far away. Generations later some descendants were brought back.

However, an amazing thing happened to the people of

this land. You would think that when times were prosperous they would have praised and worshiped their God; and when they were conquered and exiled, they would have forgotten that same God. But in truth, the opposite happened. In prosperous times, God seemed to be assumed and forgotten. In those times of darkness and despair God was remembered, called upon, and hoped for.

As we look upon this land at the beginning of the Christian era, we see a people whose history had very little of that freedom, independence, and nationhood for which they longed. Instead, we see a people struggling for existence itself. They were influenced by their former Greek conquerors, dominated by Romans, and ruled by the vicious King Herod. Herod was a sick, aged, suspicious, insanely jealous king. For political reasons, he had murdered many people, including his son and other relatives. Emperor Augustus had said ironically that he would rather be Herod's pig than his son—there would be a greater chance of survival. Herod knew how much he was hated, and so he ordered that when he died a large number of other people be put to death. He wanted *someone* mourning when he died!

Quite understandably, many persons in this land thought God had forgotten them. They had also given up any hope of their own. Still some lived with the prayer that the God of their ancestors would touch the earth once more and bring deliverance to those in bondage. They waited and hoped and prayed.

One unforgettable night their prayer was answered. For a glorious moment, heaven touched earth, but in a different way than they may have expected.

It was not in proud Jerusalem, but in obscure little Bethlehem. It did not happen among kings or priests but among simple, hard-working people usually ignored by the political and religious elite of that land.

A working-class couple sensed that the baby born to Mary was God's act of salvation and deliverance and so named him Joshua, or Jesus. On the job, shepherds were startled *to see angels*, hear them sing, and receive their announcement of this birth. Foreigners, beckoned by an unusual, intriguing star, converged on this same couple with the same excitement and commitment to God's new happening.

And though the star and the angel glow faded, the divine presence did not. "The child grew and became strong, filled with wisdom; and the favor of God was upon him" (Luke 2:40).

This land was home to him. He sweat under its sun, slept under its stars, relaxed in its oases. He fished in its lakes and bathed in its rivers. He hewed its logs, planted and raised its seeds, observed its farmers and shepherds at their work. He hiked on its hillsides, seeing in the free-flying birds of the air and the delicate spring flowers the signs of God's presence and care.

When a full-grown man, he burst into a brief but glorious ministry. He helped caring, everyday folk to think about God, and aided religious folk in showing their love. He taught the prideful to recognize their sin and encouraged prostitutes to experience forgiveness and new life. He called rich tax collectors to give up tax collecting in favor of the riches of love and commitment. He fed the hungry and awakened hungers in the satisfied that they had never known before. He helped the sick and diseased to experience wholeness and offered them even more—the wholeness of right relationship with God. He comforted the afflicted and afflicted the comfortable. He proclaimed God's rule and taught how to live in that kingdom.

He did all this all in a blazing rush, with many wanting so much from him in too short a time. He did it in a land where people paid too many taxes and had very little left over. He did it in a country that was a tinder box of revolution just waiting to explode, where paranoid leaders saw anyone who was popular, strong, or controversial as a threat.

Soon they would no longer tolerate the freedom of such a dynamic presence, and they seized him and put him to death. But he elevated even that to an act of forgiveness and sacrificial love for the world.

He died, rose, and is alive. He appeared to his followers first to give them courage and strength, and then to send them as witnesses in all the world. His executioners did not know they had set him free, so that he could promise to be there ahead of every person who went into the world to tell the gospel. And so it is that he who never traveled more than 100 miles from the place of his birth is now king of the ends of the earth.

Though I still want to visit that land again someday, I realize that the greatest importance is not that he came to that land, but that he came to earth. He shared the precarious existence of all of us. We rejoice not only that he claimed the loyalty of the people in that land, but that he is Lord of every place, time, and person, including the reader and the writer in this moment even now.

That is the story of the land and the person—a root out of dry ground.

> Joy to the world, the Lord is come,
> let earth receive her king!

TWO BIRTHS, TWO BOYS, TWO MEN

Elderly, but fairly spritely, man walks out, center stage. Two children run and greet him. He holds one and talks with the other—wordlessly in pantomime, showing delight and joy in what they have to tell him. They wave good-bye to him and run back to their place in the audience. His eyes follow them back to their seats, waving as they go. He smiles, pauses.

Ah, what a delight, what a delight! Whenever you meet a child, treat that child with wonder and reverence. For one day, that child may be your leader, your guide, your savior! Believe me, I know, I—(*senses he is being interrupted*) What did you say? Who am I? I'm . . . it really doesn't matter. Oh well, my name's Bezaleel, after the famous craftsman who helped build the tabernacle. Like Joseph I worked with my hands—used to, before these bones got so stiff. I am Elizabeth's cousin and therefore Mary's . . . oh, it's all too complicated to explain; I am kin to both. What's important is that two little boys used to call me Uncle Bez. You can call me Uncle Bez if you wish, lots of people do.

I love to sit in the quiet part of the day and think about those two boys. Folks say I make a pest of myself about them. If you listen long enough, I'll tell you about two births of two boys and the men they became.

How different those two were! One's mother was so old, and the other's mother was so very young. One was an only child, and the other was the firstborn of a large family. One loved to be alone, and the other wanted to be with people often. One seemed so full of wrath on the outside, though he had a very gentle heart. The other appeared so gentle and loving, although he had a very stern aspect to him. Oh, I'm sorry. Forgive this rambling old man, I haven't even told you their names. Their names were so important, for God guided the parents in the naming of these children. One was John—that name means "God is gracious." The other was Jesus—meaning "God is salvation." The first was termed "John the Baptizer." They spoke of the second as "Jesus of Nazareth" or "Jesus, the Christ."

(*He pauses and then walks, as if in thought. When he speaks again, he is reliving the experiences. He seats himself on a stool and looks more above people and at the ground, deeper in thought now.*)

I remember so well how excited all of the relatives were about these births. Elizabeth and Zechariah were so old—childless and barren. They were deeply sad about that. But one day, when Zechariah was on duty at the temple—he was a priest of the division of Abijah, you know—the lot fell on him to burn the incense. And while praying, a messenger of the Almighty told poor old Zechariah that, not only was he going to have a son, but the son would be great before the Lord, filled with the Holy Spirit. He would turn many of the sons of Israel to the Lord their God! (*He chuckles.*) Old Zechariah trusted God through all the disappointments, but he couldn't seem to believe this good news. As some sort of discipline, the angel struck him dumb till the time of the child's birth. When his term of service was over, he went home, and sure enough, in due time Elizabeth conceived. The miracle of Abraham and Sarah all over again, but in our day. We thought that surely it would be as the messenger told Zechariah, that this child would live in the power and spirit of the great Elijah.

For Mary, it was different. She was young, looking forward to being married and hoping for a peaceful life away from all the politics and fighting. But then God's messenger—same one, for all I know—came to Mary to commission her to bear a child who would be great, son of the Most High, to reign over the house of Jacob forever. And then in a dream, the messenger persuaded Joseph to accept her and support her in this great task. And so, for all her life, she was thrust into the middle of all the turmoil that would surround her great son.

In her fear and lonely anticipation, she came to see Elizabeth. You see Elizabeth is her kinswoman—oh, I already told you that we are all related. These two women were such a support and comfort to each other. I used to run errands for them, carry water for them. Usually women carry the water, pregnant or not! But great things were happening, and we couldn't take any chances. They thanked me for my kindness and promised me then that I could be "Uncle Bez" to their children. Truthfully, I wanted to be close to the great events happening among us and to the encouragement they felt in each other's presence. All too soon, Mary returned to her home.

When word came that Elizabeth's time had come, we kin and neighbors gathered in the courtyard of their home to wait for news. After what seemed a long time, the midwife announced that a strong, healthy son had been born. How we rejoiced that the Lord had shown them this favor. We celebrated into the night playing music, singing, and dancing. Eight days later, at the baby's circumcision, friends thought they would name him Zechariah junior! Elizabeth insisted, however, that he should be called John. They asked Zechariah and he wrote on a table, "His name is John." Then his tongue was loosed, and his first words were ecstatic praise of God. We all were filled with awe. And as we turned these matters over in our hearts, we wondered, "What is this child's future going to be?"

(*Another pause, change in expression*)

If Mary's pregnancy was frightening, her delivery was worse! There was that terrible forced journey, taxes that they could barely afford to pay, and then the labor pains came on. Joseph felt helpless and afraid. No family or friends with them in their makeshift quarters. Finally through the kindness of women at the inn she was aided and delivered.

And then, as they told me, God himself provided the party! Shepherds came. Stars shone, heavenly choruses sang, and strange learned astrologers from distant lands came bowing low and offering beautiful and costly gifts. Only when all the excitement was over did it occur to them that this might have been part of the Almighty's plan—to have the promised one born in David's city, Bethlehem. After a hasty detour to escape a murderous king, they returned to Nazareth, where the baby would live his childhood and youthful years.

I had never noticed how quickly the years passed until I measured them by the growth of those two boys. Though I lived close to Zechariah and saw John often, for a time, I only saw Jesus every two or three years when his parents were able to save enough to come to a temple festival and stop off for a few days' visit. It's a long way from Galilee to Judea—a hard, two-day walk for a man, much more than that for a woman or child. Those visits were very special times. Sometimes I took those two boys on hikes up in these Judean hills. I'd overhear their conversations; both mothers had told them that they were children promised of God. But what that meant they did not know. Only time would reveal—God's time. They enjoyed every discovery, a tiny flower, a cactus. Even then, John was off by himself a good bit. And he never wanted to leave, even when the sun was low and the evening meal would soon be offered. Ah, what great times those were.

Too soon the sadness came. First Zechariah died and then Elizabeth—both of them full of years. Then Joseph died, when that beam fell on him. John was left alone, and to Jesus fell the responsibility of being the eldest son in a large family of little hungry mouths. For years he worked hard at supporting them and feeding them. On the other hand, John was taken to that monastery down by the Dead Sea, where they live simply and teach righteousness and have a very rigid daily discipline. He stayed there for a little while, but then he left and was alone—up there in those hills in the wilderness.

And time passed. I did not see either of them for years. My beard became grey and my joints stiffened. I waited and wondered what our God was going to do next through those boys.

Then, one day it happened. I had almost given up hope when I heard the news that a mighty prophet had appeared in the wilderness by the river Jordan. I can't get around as fast as I used to, but I had to go see. It was as I suspected, my little John, now a power-filled spokesman for God! I could see what had happened. Out in the desert, he got down to basics. He lived off the wilderness, eating seeds and roots and locusts and wild honey. His clothes, too, were simple—a rough garment of camel's hair with a leather girdle around his waist. God's sun had burned all the dross out of his soul. God's wind had blown all the chaff away. When God told him the time was *now*, a power filled him and he saw with clearer vision what was central and basic and true. But even more, God told him of the dawning of a new age. It was no wonder that crowds gathered to hear him, for he spoke to a hunger, an emptiness in all of us.

He cried out, "Repent, turn around, change your ways,

for the kingdom of heaven is at hand." To overly pious religious leaders, he said, "You nest of snakes! Who warned you to flee from the wrath to come as the animals race before a grass fire? Do something to show that your lives are really changed. And don't trust in the fact that you are Abraham's descendants. God can make more out of these stones. God doesn't care where you came from. God is concerned with where you are going. Come to the waters with me. As the heathen are baptized when they become part of our people of Israel, so you must come and be baptized to be cleansed and made right with God, truly God's chosen people."

As fast as these old legs could carry me, I was one of the first in the water with him. He recognized me, and his eyes twinkled. However, he said nothing but, "I baptize you with water. One is coming who will baptize you with the Holy Spirit and with fire." The Jordan is a muddy river, but I felt so clean and alive and full of hope as I walked out of it. As soon as I got the grit out of my eyes, I saw a world more full of hope, more full of God than I had ever seen before.

Shortly after that, there was a most significant day. Since I was not there, others told me of it. Jesus appeared over the rise, and slowly but directly walked to John, who was standing in the water. Rarely was John at a loss for words, but he was that day." I . . . I need to be baptized by you, and you come to me?" he asked. They had not seen each other for years, but John's clear spiritual vision saw that Jesus was the one of whom he had been speaking. Jesus responded simply, "Let it be so. It is fitting that we do each righteous act that God requires." John later told folks. "When I baptized him, I heard the thunder and saw the fire descend on him, the lamb of God." Jesus simply remembered, "I saw the heavens opened. The Spirit of God descended on me like a dove, and my Father called out, 'This is my beloved son, on whom my favor rests.'"

After this, Jesus immediately went out into that same wilderness to pray, listen, and prepare. And while he was out there, tragedy struck! John had spoken a little too bluntly that Herod should not have stolen his half-brother's wife and divorced his own. One night after the crowds left, Herod's soldiers came and led John away. They took that freedom-craving man who loved the outdoors so much and shut him up in a windowless dungeon cell in that palace fort called Machaerus, down by the Dead Sea. Only his strong God must have kept him from suffocating in there.

There were some things that kept him going. For one thing, Herod himself would repeatedly call him up to talk. Herod heard him gladly, but was much perplexed. Herod knew John was a righteous and holy man, but he did not comprehend where John obtained his power. Over and over again they discussed it. John could not quite convince Herod, nor could Herod dismiss the truths John stated to him. The other thing that sustained John was that some of his disciples were allowed to visit once in a while. He loved his time with them, and they kept him informed about what was happening outside. When they told of Jesus' ministry, John was somewhat troubled. It didn't sound the way he had envisioned it.

Jesus had set about a ministry of proclaiming God's reign: teaching, training, feeding, helping, healing—so many things. Even greater crowds came to him, so many in fact, that he had a hard time getting away and resting. Being somewhat curious, I had gone to see him, also. And I could see why John was puzzled. Jesus' ministry had power, but it was a quieter, gentler power. He wasn't laying the ax to the tree as John had predicted, at least not yet.

And so John sent his disciples to ask, "Are you the one who is to come, or shall we look for someone else?" When John's disciples came, Jesus did not directly answer their question. He almost never did. Instead, he responded "Tell John what you see. Blind folks are becoming bird watchers. Cripples are throwing away their crutches. Lepers are becoming clean and restored to their families. Deaf folks are able to discard their listening trumpets. Indeed, the dead are coming back to life. And happy is the one who never loses faith in me."

Then Jesus asked the crowd, "What did you go out to the desert to see? A shaking reed? No? A luxuriously dressed man? Of course not. You went to see a prophet and more—the one whom scripture describes as a messenger who shall prepare the way. I tell you that among those born of women, no one is greater than John. And yet, he who is least in the kingdom of God is greater than he." Some gasped at that statement, but John would have understood—John predicted God's kingdom. In Jesus, it was here!

Then Jesus added a playful joke. "But I can't figure you folks out," he said. "You are like children; and yet you wouldn't play 'funeral' with John and you won't play 'wedding' with me. For John came eating no bread and drinking no wine, and you say he is crazy. Then I came enjoying life, and you say, 'He's a drunkard and a glutton, a pal of tax collectors and other sinners.' " (*Bezaleel smiles and chuckles a little, walks a bit, and then turns very somber.*)

I am an old man, and I expected to go to my grave much sooner than these young men; but it was not to be so. There is such pain in losing our young men, particularly to violent deaths!

John was probably doomed from the moment he was imprisoned. Herodias—Herod's wife, if you can call her that—resented John for what he said about her relationship with Herod. She was a plotting, evil woman. Finally she found her way. One year, Herod threw a birthday party for himself. Late in the evening, when all were quite drunk, Herodias sent her daughter, Salome, in to dance for Herod. Herod was so pleased that he offered her anything she wanted. And prompted by her mother, she asked for the head of John the Baptist! Wily old Herod was trapped by his promise. For a filthy pagan dance, he killed that magnificent man of God!

John's disciples came and buried his body. When they told Jesus, he went away to a deserted place to mourn and to pray.

Jesus' death was strange. As his followers later recalled, he seemed to know it was coming and spoke of it; but at the time they denied that such a thing could happen. Then he started a journey straight toward his worst enemies in Jerusalem. His disciples did not abandon him, but they followed, trembling, they said. But in Jerusalem, it appeared that things really fell apart. One betrayed him, one denied him, and all ran and hid for their own safety. Strangers and enemies took him over, convicted him on false charges, beat him brutally, and *crucified* him. The person we loved, all that he stood for, all that we hoped for, died up there on that cross that day. It felt like more than our breaking hearts could bear.

However, I am now coming to see that God was not defeated, not even in those two untimely deaths. For the message of righteousness and repentance that John preached lives on even after his death. It is said that his ghost still haunts old Herod and befuddles Herod's efforts. John's disciples tell his story, and people are still touched by the life of that man.

And Jesus! Just a few days after his death, his disciples discovered that the grave could not hold him. He came back to life! He walked among them, instructed them, commissioned them to tell his story to the ends of the earth, and empowered them. I was not among those who saw him in the days of his appearing. But I have visited with his followers and felt their power. I followed my heart and believe that this Jesus is indeed the promised one of God.

Some time ago, he was asked, "Can a man be born again when he is old?" I now know the answer to that question. I am old, but my faith is young. I am alive!

(*Looks up at sun*) Oh me, is it that late already? I'm afraid I bored you. What was I saying? Oh yes:

Treat each child with love and reverence; you never know who that child will become. I used to take two little boys hiking up in the hills. One became my spiritual leader. The other is my Savior and Lord! Shalom! (*Waves good-bye and leaves*)

TO THEOPHILUS,
WITH LOVE

Luke sits at desk, writing. He talks to himself, adds, crosses out, tries to improve.

"Write their own story," no, "compile a narrative." Yes, that sounds better. . . . Let's see, "that you may be better informed," no, that's too weak. "That you may know the truth." That has a nice ring to it. I think I've finally put this the way I want to.

(*Picks up scrap and reads*) "Inasmuch as many have undertaken to compile a narrative of the things which have been accomplished among us, just as they were delivered to us by those who from the beginning were eyewitnesses and ministers of the word, it seemed good to me also, having followed all things closely for some time past, to write an orderly account for you, most excellent Theophilus, that you may know the truth concerning the things of which you have been informed." Ah, at last, my first paragraph of the book I am writing for you, Theophilus. I hope that these words reflect, in some small way, the majesty of what I have to tell you. It feels so good to write that first paragraph.

Only, what do I do now? Where do I begin to tell you the story burning in my heart, the story I so want for you to have as your own? I have such little space to tell you the story. This scroll, when full, will only hold the tales I could tell you in an evening. And I could talk to you about this person for days and days! I have read what there is to read, talked to those who were near, and I have so much to tell you!

Maybe I will write two scrolls for you instead of one. Yes, that's it. In the first I can tell you what he did in his days on this earth. In the second I can go on to say what he did through his Spirit in spreading the good news to the ends of the earth. I can tell so much more that way.

But even then, I can reveal only the tiniest part. Oh, how I hope he will live for you through my mere words in this scroll. I want you to know how gentle and caring he was—especially to women and children. May you sense his healing power and compassion for the suffering. I want to tell you about the power of silence and prayer in his life. Most of all I want you to know that though he was first seen as the promised one for the Jewish people, he came for all of us. In him there is love, joy, peace, and life everlasting.

And I must say this in just a few cubits of scroll. All I will be able to do is choose some of the finest stories about him—oh, yes, and some of those marvelous tales he told, and hope that the truth shines through. May it be that your heart communicates with my heart far beyond the brief stories I will be able to put on the page.

I keep delaying for fear that I cannot do justice to my great theme. Almighty God, bless and inspire me as I attempt to tell the story of your son and servant who walked among us and blessed us. In his name, Amen.

Though my words pale in insignificance in trying to express the mighty theme of which I will write, it's time to begin. But at what point in the story should I start? Mark began his account with Jesus as a full grown man, responding to John the Baptist's preaching, being baptized, and being tempted.

Though Mark has taught me much, I think I must start with the promise and the birth. Do I dare take space on this scroll for these stories? I must, for there is something about a child that touches the heart. And this child stirs me deeply.

I must speak of the promise and of two births. In the fullness of time strange events began to occur. God's messengers roamed the earth, encountering those whom God chose and recruiting them for roles in the divine drama of salvation.

This all began in the days of Herod, king of Judea. I will place this story within the history of the age. (*Gesturing toward an imaginary stack of scrolls*.) There are many documents to tell me of the emperors, the governors, the kings, the military campaigns, the battles. The one of whom I speak was unnoticed by all of these for much of his life. He was like an almost invisible golden thread binding together heaven and earth, present struggles and future promises. He bound us to each other in love. I will speak of the emperors, but mostly of this golden thread called Jesus. This is how I will begin. . . .

(*Writing words on scroll, then pausing to reflect*) "In the days of Herod, king of Judea, there was a priest named Zechariah"—a layman priest, who twice a year took time off from his work to go with his division, the division of Abijah, to enter into the priestly assembly at the temple. During one of those times "it fell to him by lot to enter the temple of the Lord and burn incense"—perhaps the first time in his entire life that this honor came to him. It was an unforgettable day, soon to become even more so. "The whole multitude of the people were praying outside at the hour of incense. And there appeared to him an angel of the Lord standing on the right side of the altar of incense." Nothing like this had ever happened, and Zechariah was afraid. But the messenger told him that his wife and he—aged as they were—would have a son who would be important in the Lord's service. The messenger said that they should call him John, a name that means "God is gracious." Although a devout man, Zechariah was skeptical; and he came from there stricken of voice.

However, in time, the promise was kept and Elizabeth conceived. It was the story of Abraham and Sarah, of Elkanah and Hannah all over again. Here was a sign that God was beginning something strange and wonderful.

The mysterious events heralding the dawn of a new age were but beginning. In the sixth month of Elizabeth's pregnancy, "the angel Gabriel was sent from God to a city of Galilee named Nazareth." Nazareth! What a strange place for an angel to come! Oh, the setting in the Galilean hills is pretty enough, but it was a nondescript town like so many others. If I had not mentioned it to you, Theophilus, you probably would never have heard of it. The messenger came to "a virgin betrothed to a man whose name was Joseph, of the house of David; and the virgin's name was Mary. And he came to her and said, 'Hail, O favored one, the Lord is with you!'" Mary was troubled and confused, wondering what sort of greeting that might be. She was told not to be afraid for she had found favor with God.

Up to this point in her life, Mary had hoped for little more than a peaceful home with Joseph, to whom she was promised. Somehow, she wanted their home to be a haven, shut off from the struggles, revolution, and brutality that raged around them. She would have liked to have escaped the cruelty of the age. All this was to be denied her with the next word of the angel. "And behold, you will conceive in your womb and bear a son, and you shall call his name Jesus. He will be great, and will be called the Son of the Most High; and the Lord God will give to him the throne of his father David, and he will reign over the house of Jacob forever; and of his kingdom there will be no end."

Mary, like Zechariah, struggled to believe this was really happening. She asked incredulously, "How can this be?" And the messenger responded, "The Holy Spirit will come upon you, and the power of the Most High will overshadow you; therefore the child to be born will be called holy, the Son of God."

To her credit and to the glory of God, Theophilus, this gracious young woman overcame her fears and resistances. She simply responded, " 'Behold, I am the handmaid of the Lord; let it be to me according to your word.' And the angel departed from her," and it was so.

Deeply troubled, Mary went with haste to the hill country of Judea to her kinswoman Elizabeth and spent three months with her. Only with her could secrets be shared, fears faced, and hopes spoken out loud. Then she returned to her now turbulent life in Nazareth. Shortly after she returned, she received the marvelous word that her kinswoman had given birth and that the child was strong and healthy. They had named him John, and at that point, father Zechariah's tongue was loosed to praise the Lord. Those around were struck with wonder at these events and asked, "What then will this child be?" Only a few knew the answer to that, even in the smallest part.

Mary's life had returned to almost normal, when another event shook them. "In those days a decree went out from Caesar Augustus that all the world should be enrolled. This was the first enrollment, when Quirinius was governor of Syria." (*As he says this, he checks facts in imaginary scroll.*) Enrolled? Taxed is a better word. No one likes taxes. Some raised voices in protest. But Roman soldiers' clubs and swords quieted the resistance very quickly. "And all went to be enrolled, each to his own city. And Joseph also went up from Galilee from the city of Nazareth, to Judea, to the city of David, which is called Bethlehem, because he was of the house and lineage of

David, to be enrolled with Mary his betrothed, who was with child." They walked across Galilean hills to Lake Galilee, down the Jordan valley, to the warm, deep incline at Jericho. Then there was the long, slow climb to Jerusalem, and finally up a hill and down over the small road to Bethlehem, just a short distance to the southeast of Jerusalem. Vigorous men can walk that journey in two or three days. For them, it took much longer. Joseph was a builder, a practical and capable man, a man of few words. However, this journey stretched even his abilities to provide. Would his beloved miscarry along the way? Would this journey be the death of his Mary and the child? How he worried and fretted. At last, dirty, exhausted, and frightened, they reached Bethlehem. In their strain they had missed an irony now visible to our eyes. A hated Roman decree about taxes had led them to Bethlehem, where the hope of the nations could be born in the city of David!

However, having finally reached their destination, their problems were not over. "The time came for her to be delivered. And she gave birth to her first-born son and wrapped him in swaddling cloths, and laid him in a manger, because there was no place for them in the inn."

At times, Theophilus, there is an awful loneliness about this story. Far removed from family, friends, and even their simple home, Mary gave birth. The king of the ends of the earth was born on the earth, literally, and placed in a manger.

However, this loneliness was to end rather shortly. Almighty God was about to provide unknown friends to come and celebrate the birth. For once again, God sent angels—messengers—to give news that the birth had taken place. These messengers came upon a field near where a band of shepherds cared for sheep. They may have been caring for lambs intended for sacrifices in the temple; the one they were told about would be the lamb of God, one day taking away the sins of the world. To these shepherds was given news of the birth of one who would be *their* shepherd. Then the angels did the only thing they could do to express such news: they sang, "Glory to God in the highest, and on earth peace among those with whom he is pleased!" And, Theophilus, ever since, this birth has inspired songs and singing without end.

The shepherds acted on the announcement, came to Bethlehem "with haste, and found Mary and Joseph, and the babe lying in a manger. And when they saw it they made known the saying which had been told them concerning the child; and all who heard it wondered at what the shepherds told them. But Mary kept all these things, pondering them in her heart." Too soon, the shepherds knew they must give attention to their flocks and returned to their work, thanking and praising God for what they had heard and seen.

On the eighth day the child was circumcised and they called him Jesus, meaning "God is salvation," the name given him by the angel before he was conceived.

When the child was forty days old, they took him to the temple in Jerusalem for the purification rites. And while there, they were recognized by two old people. These folks' eyes had grown dim with age, yet they could see what others could not—the golden thread this child was to be. There were many children brought that day. Mary and Joseph were among the poorer of the families; indeed, they gave the offering of the poor, "a pair of turtledoves or two young pigeons," because they could not afford the customary lamb. But somehow the aged Simeon knew, took the child in his arms, blessed God, and prayed, "Lord, now lettest thou thy servant depart in peace, according to thy word; for mine eyes have seen thy salvation." With a gentle word to Mary about the pain that would come as the mother of such a child, he handed the baby back. At that moment, an aged prophetess, Anna, came up and gave thanks to God for the fulfillment she recognized in the child. Even Joseph and Mary marveled at what was said to them about the child.

"And when they had performed everything according to the law of the Lord, they returned into Galilee, to their own city, Nazareth. And the child grew and became strong, filled with wisdom; and the favor of God was upon him."

Well, Theophilus, that's the beginning—perhaps you now see why I had to speak of the children and of the faithful folks who welcomed them. Our spiritual father Paul once said that "God chose what is foolish in the world to shame the wise, God chose what is weak in the world to shame the strong, God chose what is low and despised in the world, even things that are not, to bring to nothing things that are." His words are true about this story. When God, in the fullness of time, began a new age, he did so through simple faithful folk who welcomed and cared for these children.

I must stop writing for a while—my eyes burn and my hand aches. I will write more soon.

While Caesars made decrees and governors taxed and regiments patrolled, two little boys played and grew. One was called John, "God is gracious," and the other was Jesus, "God is salvation." God was about the shake the world and bring about a new beginning through them.

O Theophilus, lover of God, excellency, how I hope you will serve, love, and be shaped by this Jesus. I have become his follower and am ever being molded in his likeness.

I am,

Your obedient servant,

Luke

94

THE MYSTERIOUS CELEBRATION

Don't ask me why it happened! Look, I'm no electronics expert. I don't understand why these gizmos work, why they don't work, or why they do something different than they're supposed to. All I know is that somehow these messages came in on my receiver and appeared from time to time on my printer. At first, I thought it was some prank by the guys down in advertising. However, I soon became convinced that this one was beyond them. I had a feeling these unexplained communiqués might be something important, and so I stuck them in a file folder. Here is some of what appeared on my printer. This first one appeared on November 25.

"Commander, I arrived without incident at the small planet to which you assigned me. Using the plastic card included in the basic equipment you issued, I secured a headquarters room quite quickly. Then, as directed, I began observing. The people of this planet seem to be a friendly and intelligent folk. Oh, there are some differences that are hard to get used to. Instead of our efficient three fingers on each hand, they have five. I can't see that the extra fingers are any use, except for their specially designed musical instruments and to wear decorations. Their heads are not pointed, like ours, but rather oval. And they are not hairless, as we. Instead, they have a good bit of body hair, especially on the tops of their heads. Rather than being ashamed of this, they are rather vain about it. They color it, twist it, and tie it in a variety of ways.

"Their customs are rather different also. When they meet persons, they interlock fingers, or hold each other close, not nudge shoulders as we do. And when they feel tender toward another, they do not caress elbows as we do. They join their mouths together!

"I must sign off for now to continue investigating. Please greet Mara and tell her I can't wait to hold her in my elbows."

The next one was dated about a week later, December 1.

"Commander, something strange is going on. Lights are springing out everywhere—tall buildings and small homes, all over. The marketplaces are becoming even more beautiful. Huge crowds come to the shopping places, more every day. People buy things urgently. At first, I thought they were stocking up to prepare for some catastrophe, but there seems to be little fear. People are still friendly, but I can't seem to ask the right questions. I ask, 'What's going on? Why are we doing this? Why are things changing?' and people just laugh, or stare at me. These are the same people who will say hello, or give directions to a new place quite freely. I am puzzled, but I will keep investigating."

The next day, another brief communiqué appeared. December 2.

"Commander, I have learned a new technique. I go to one of the food rooms in the shopping place, eat my food slowly, and listen to what persons at the other tables are saying. Today, I heard a woman next to me say, 'I am halfway through my list.' I looked over her shoulder and saw a list of names. I guess they are buying all these goods to be gifts for many persons known to them. Why, I do not know. But I will keep listening."

Next day, December 3. Another message appeared.

"Commander. At my listening table in the food place, I received another important clue. I heard a person mutter, "Oh me, he really started something when he was born, didn't he!' Of course! All this extra activity must be around the birth of some great leader! I wandered through the marketplace (they call them shopping malls here) to find some clue as to whose birth we are celebrating. There were no clear answers, but from what I saw, here are some possible hypotheses:

"Perhaps we are celebrating the birth of Thomas Edison, inventor of the light bulb, by letting there be no dark corners any more.

"Perhaps we are celebrating the birth of these people's popular national leader. By watching the late movies in my motel room, I discern that he might have been born in the barn on a set of one of his western movies.

"Perhaps we note the birth of one S. Nicholas or S. Claus. There seem to be different forms of the name. If I catch the music in the shopping place, this S. Claus was born in an igloo in the Arctic regions. Persons seeking him were guided by the nose of a reindeer. And all who came to see him were turned into elves.

"I am not sure, but I will keep looking. It is all so confusing. Give Mara a nudge on the shoulder for me, and tell her that better days are coming when I finish this assignment."

This little creature must have been hard at work, for there was another report intercepted in my printer the very next day. Let me read it.

"Of all the earth people I have met, I most enjoy a young woman who serves tables at the food room where I often go. Her name is Sally, and I think she must have one of the most difficult jobs on earth. Sometimes people are in such a hurry. Occasionally they are upset, and at times they want so much attention. She treats them all well, with kindness and respect. There is a very warm feeling in her part of the eating room. I felt I could put my questions to her, and so I went in after the rush. I asked her if I could buy her some of the food she usually serves. She said she had a break coming. So she sat down for dessert, and we talked. I told her I was from out of town and so I had some questions. 'Whose birthday is it?' I asked. Kind Sally just stared at me for a minute. 'Out of town?' she said. 'Are you sure it's not from outer space?' I wondered how she knew, but I just waited. 'You're just teasing, aren't you?' She said, 'It's the birthday of the Savior.' I still did not know what to say. 'You know, Jesus.' 'Jesus who?' I asked. She looked directly into my eyes. 'You don't know, do you?' she responded. 'Look, I'm off tomorrow. Would you like to go to my church with me and hear the Christmas story?' It seemed the most promising lead I'd found, so far, especially coming from a caring person like Sally. So I accepted. I will report tomorrow on what I found."

This was getting interesting, and so I watched with interest the next day, but no report flowed through my printer. Nor the next, nor the next. I thought that maybe the same glitch that put me in touch, took me out of touch. Happily, on the fourth day, another message came through my printer, and I read with interest.

"Commander, please forgive the delay in this report. You will see in what I tell you my reasons for not transmitting sooner.

"I did go to church with Sally the next day. Church. What an odd word! Funny, I now see that there are these church buildings in many places. But they are so much smaller than the shopping places that I had hardly noticed them. We went to a beautiful assembly room. (The crowds were smaller than at the shopping places also.) There we both stood and sat. We sang and listened to others sing.

We read from their holy book. (Now I know what that black book in the dresser drawer in my room is.) One person led us in talking to their unseen God. Their leader (they called him a pastor) called the children together and spoke to them so simply that even I could understand. He told about the birth of a baby named Jesus, born to a woman named Mary, and how this child grew to be a person that brought God's love to the whole earth. Later he talked to all of us about how the story of this birth came to humble folks at their place of work. I stored all his references in my memory bank so I could look them up in the holy book back in my room.

"Then we went into another room and drank their sacred drink—I think it is called coffee. Many persons intertwined fingers, or held others close, and talked and laughed for a long time. I met Sally's grandmother, who invited me to their family Christmas party. Someone else asked me to go caroling. Sally introduced me to her minister and told him I was brand new and had lots of questions. We agreed to meet soon.

"For the first time, I did not feel so lonely on earth. I also sensed that I was getting close to solving the mysteries you sent me here to explore.

"I did go 'caroling' with some church folks. That means singing a lot of those songs I was hearing all day long in the shopping places. We went to some places where sickly older persons stayed and sang our songs. How beautiful it was. They knew the songs too, and they sang them with us. They waved and smiled and cried. There was lots of hand-holding and hugging. Somehow we who were strangers were drawn very close together by the songs about the one born at Christmas.

"My visit with the pastor was . . ." (Here the printer became erratic, slowed, and stopped. I applied the only mechanical treatment I know—I pounded it with my fists, several times, and it started slowly again. There were a few lines of jibberish, but then it picked up as follows) "I had spent hours with their holy book processing what it says about the one called Jesus. Much of it, I could easily understand, but some was beyond me. I asked the minister, 'This verse, "The word became flesh and dwelt among us, full of grace and truth." What does that mean?' The minister was quiet a few moments, searching for words. 'It means that the power and wisdom and majesty of God expressed itself in human flesh, in Jesus Christ,' he said. I was stunned. 'Is that true?' I asked. He simply nodded. I could not contain myself. 'Then why are you folks so calm and complacent about this truth? Why are you so secretive? You act like everybody knows, and they don't! Don't you know that this is the truth the whole universe longs to hear? Don't you think that news would bring peace to the hurrying folks at the shopping place? Are you sending that message around the world?' 'A little,' the minister meekly replied. 'A little? A little?' I gasped. 'Your world is on the brink of destruction and you send a little? I would think that when the Eternal One entrusts you with the greatest truth, you would share it with everything you have!' There were tears in his eyes, but he smiled, just a bit, and said, 'You ought to preach the Christmas sermon next Sunday and tell them what you told me.' I answered him, 'I'm just beginning to learn about all this, I don't know what to say. You tell them.' There was a glint in his eye, like a commander with a new plan. 'Maybe I will,' he said."

Immediately after the communication was complete, I called the service man who cleaned, oiled, and adjusted my printer. This was none too soon, for a couple days later, another communiqué came through—this time not missing a letter.

"Commander, you sent me on a mission to earth to solve two mysteries. I can now report at least partial answers to each.

"Mystery one: What were the strange otherworldly sounds from centuries past coming from this planet that our historical sound sensor had been attempting to intercept for some time? Their holy book tells us that these were messengers from the Eternal One, singing a song of special good news. The holy book said their song was 'Glory to God in highest heaven. And on earth, God's peace for folks on whom God's favor rests.' From my experiences, that book is a reliable witness.

"Mystery two: Now that the people of this planet have discovered the destructive power of the atom, will they destroy themselves, as have some planets, with this knowledge? Or will they learn how to live together in peace? That is very hard to know, Excellency. They have the truth, the person who could bind them together. But they ignore both the truth bringer, and the urgency of their situation. I do not know at this time if they will claim their truth and make it known in order to bind themselves together in peace. I know that is the prayer of many people. But its progress seems slow indeed. We should monitor this planet closely to see what comes of this dilemma.

"Commander, I cannot lie to you. I must share one more part of my experience with that minister. There was another verse in the same chapter of the holy book that read, 'He came unto his own and his own received him not. But as many as received him, to them he gave the power to become the children of God, even to them that believed on his name; who were born not of blood nor of the will of the flesh, nor of the will of man, but of God.' I asked him what that meant. He told me that persons could open their lives to God's presence and power to transform their views and their relationships. You just had to ask, he said, 'It is like being born anew to the living presence of God.'

'Like Sally and her grandmother?' I asked.

'Yes,' he said, 'they are two of our clearest examples.' I remembered that I had once asked Sally why she was so kind. 'Because of the love of my family, my church, and my Lord,' she had said. This seemed to me to be the most important clue of all. I cannot understand their power unless I am within it. The minister said that I just need to ask. And so I did, and I do, and I will. And sure enough, I do sense some of God's peace and love in me. There's a long way to go, but something is stirring. I return to you as one of us and also one of them.

"I delayed my voyage home one day, so that I could attend that Christmas party of Sally's family. I'm glad I went there as my last experience with earth people. It was my first time in an earth person's home and it was so friendly, warm, and bright. I could tell that they were glad of each other's existence, and they that could be together. Sally's grandmother had a gift for me. I tried to refuse it—I know she has so little, and I feared I could not take it with me. But she insisted it was especially for me, and it was. I opened it. It was a cap and gloves she had knitted. The cap had a pointed top, the gloves had three fingers. I tried them on, even though, as you know, with our inner controls we can adapt to any climate. And indeed, there was more warmth in those gifts than from the yarn alone. Impulsively I reached out to her and gave her my first earth hug, the closest I'd let myself come to anyone there. It felt good, but it made me regret that my departure was so imminent. When Sally gave me a ride home at the end of the evening, I told her I would be leaving the next morning. She softly told me that Christians need never say good-bye. They only say 'God be with you till we meet again.' But she held my hand tightly for a long time. It was hard to let go and watch her drive off in the darkness. There is something of magnetism and majesty about these earth people who are followers. I can see why the Almighty loves them so.

"This is my last message from earth. Tomorrow I begin my voyage home. I will bring the sacred book, my memory banks, and a changing heart. We will have important times, discussing these exciting truths. Perhaps within these teachings there is hope for our planet as well. Tell Mara I come to her soon, and that along with all my love and longing for her, I bring to her the Christian way of loving as well. What times of joy there will be. It will be more than worth waiting for."

And then, with a close-off code, it was gone. As I suspected, though I've kept the printer oiled and clean, it has not printed any messages again. I leave it on, though, just in case. Funny, I never saw this hairless guy with the little pointed head, or even learned his name; but when the messages stopped, I felt as though I'd lost my best friend.

Sometimes on a clear starry night I stand outside and think. From somewhere out there in those stars, a messenger came to us and a missionary went out from us. I dare to believe and hope that, who knows, the end of the story may be even better than its beginning.

CHILDREN OF PEACE

Gerald Hamilton, U.S. State Department, closed the door and gulped two more aspirin. He wearily sank into his chair, as he took a well-deserved five-minute break. Gerald glanced at the appointment list of those who were waiting outside to have their say. Good, only three more left.

Whose bright idea was this "Ask the People" project? Some higher up who didn't have to do it, he was sure. Since the peace and disarmament talks had stalled for some time, and because there was growing public criticism and unrest on this topic, someone at the State Department had said, "Ask the people." Others thought of it, but Gerald had to *do* it.

Without much enthusiasm, he had carried the idea out. He ran modest ads in a few newspapers. The ads offered any citizen fifteen minutes to talk to a State Department official. The purpose was to gather suggestions for breaking the stalemate in the international peace discussion.

The response was more than he had feared it would be. For two weeks he had listened for more than eight hours a day. And what had he heard? Nothing useful, as far as he could tell. The clichés, the anti-American propaganda, the already tried and failed ideas, the generalizations—what a waste, what an exhausting waste of time. On his desk was a huge pile of prepared statements that various persons had left—statements he knew he would never read again. Gerald was aware he had been selected for this task because he was tactful, patient, and could look interested whether he was or not. Ah well, three more dull interviews and a brief report at tomorrow's staff meeting, and this fiasco would be over. He nodded to his aide to admit the next one.

In bounced a young woman, probably in her twenties. She was holding a whimpering, wiggly baby less than a year old. On her shoulder was a good-sized bag. Scarcely looking at Gerald, she glanced about the room. Selecting the only available space, she plopped her baby on Gerald's immaculate desk and deftly began changing him and cleaning up his mess. "Here," she said, holding a closed dirty diaper in one hand and a bottle in the other, while at the same time confining the baby to the desk with an elbow. "Will you get rid of this and run some warm water over the bottle?"

"I will not!" Gerald answered coldly.

"OK, fine. Here, then," she responded, thrusting the baby into his hands, as she disappeared into the bathroom. Gerald, a neat, orderly bachelor, who liked it that way, tried holding the baby outside of slobbering or spitting range. The baby didn't like that, so he drew him a little closer and walked him around the office. What was taking her so long? Finally she came out of the bathroom and took her child. Sitting down and holding him close, she gave him the bottle. He drank noisily but became quiet and content.

By now Gerald was unnerved. His veneer was about to crack. "This is no nursery. Couldn't you have cared for these things before you got here?"

"What, lose my place in the line and depend on peace activists to give it back?" she responded with a grin.

"Look Ms. . . ." In all this confusion he had misplaced his list and his clipboard.

"Jan, Jan Miller," she filled in.

"Ms. Miller, just give me your prepared statement and leave."

"I don't have anything written," she responded, "I came to talk."

He snapped, "Talk, then. You have seven minutes left to say what you want."

With enthusiasm and straightforwardness, Jan told about an idea that had been developing in her mind ever since Billy had been born. In spite of himself, Gerald found himself caught up in her excitement. So much so, that he allowed her to talk past her time limit, for a minute or two. Then he rose and ushered her out—making sure she didn't leave behind her diaper bag. After she left, he mused that this was the first original idea he'd heard in these dozens of appointments.

The next day at staff meeting, he was scheduled to report on the project "Ask the People." His department head cut him short on any long summary and asked curtly, "Anything worthwhile come of this?"

"Just one idea, as far as I could tell. I met a young mother—and her baby. She says that disarmament negotiations should be conducted with a child present!" After a few guffaws and snickers, he continued. "She has offered to come to future negotiating sessions and bring her child."

"Of course. I supposed she wants to go on the payroll and expense account."

"No. She said she would pay her own expense. Her grandmother left her a small bequest, and she feels her grandma would want her to use it to dream and to risk."

"She probably plans to make a bundle on publicity. Endorsements . . . first-person stories for the tabloids."

Gerald again responded, "She promised that there would be none of that. I can get it in writing."

"What conditions did she demand or request?"

"Only that she know the schedule well in advance to arrange for employment leave. She works evenings as a waitress so that she can spend the days with Billy."

"If we have one, the Russians will insist that they have one, too."

"Her idea was that we suggest it."

The department head shook his head and sighed. "The press is clamoring to know what came of Project 'Ask the People.' I guess if that's what you have, we better go with it. Run a security check on her. If she clears, we'll give it a try."

Thus it was that a simple, modest change came about in the disarmament negotiations. On the roster of consultants and observers, there were two names that were identified as "peace mothers": Jan Miller and Katherine Kamerov. There were also two names that were described as "children of peace": Billy Miller and Natasha Kamerov.

The ground rules were basic. At the convening session of each round of negotiations, each mother and child would greet the head of the other nation. The mother could offer a two-sentence, noncontroversial greeting. Then mothers and children were to sit in the front row of the consultants' section, in full view of the negotiators. Children were to sit on mothers' laps or play quietly on the floor at their feet. If they became noisy or disruptive, they were to leave until parent and child were ready to return.

Those were the official ground rules. Of course, during the course of the three years, the children stretched them. They were able to run under the security rope. Very quickly they became favorites of the two heads of state. Quite on his own, Billy started calling the Russian leader "Uncle Nicki"—to his great delight. Natasha, always quick to catch on, called the American leader "Uncle President." When these august leaders arrived each morning, the children would squeal with delight, wriggle out of their mothers' arms and run over, and expect a hug, a little song, or a quick game. They were rarely disappointed. Shortly the children were escorted back to their mothers. Then the business of the day proceeded as usual.

And so it went. For the next three years they met every several months, about twice a year, in various cities of the world—usually in Europe. Always Katherine and Natasha, Jan and Billy, sat in the front row. Each day there were brief, warm greetings for the children, then long, involved negotiations.

As the process went on, Jan was unsure that she had been right. She knew how much her grandma hated war; she had lost a husband in one and had risked a son (Jan's father) in another. She recalled how Grandma was a peacemaker, a healer in every relationship she could touch. How Jan wished that Grandma had lived long enough to see Billy. What a relief it would be to call her right now! When Jan made her proposal, it was the only way she could think of to use Grandma's bequest to do what she believed in. She hoped this was not a useless venture.

What had been accomplished by the mothers and children being there for all these discussions? In these three years of meetings, Jan could recognize a few things of real importance. For one thing, she and Katherine had become close friends. They usually stayed at the same inexpensive hotel, some distance from the negotiating sites. Often they commuted together on public transportation or shared a taxi. At first, they knew but a few words of the other's language. They struggled to learn more so that they could share more and were succeeding. Jan and Katherine would relax together at the end of a long day, or one would care for both children so that the other could have a little time to herself.

Natasha and Billy had done well with each other from the start. They could communicate without words, but they learned each other's words quickly as well. What lively little peace ambassadors they were—Natasha with her coal-black hair, dark penetrating eyes, and shy melodic laughter; Billy, blond and blue-eyed, friendly and outgoing, unafraid of anything or anybody. When negotiating sessions were on, those two were inseparable. They were ingenious at inventing quiet games and activities. Such creativity enabled them to spend more nondisruptive time in the negotiating halls than anyone had imagined possible. If more people cared for each other across nationalities as Natasha and Billy did, peace would have a chance.

Then too, these mothers had met other parents and children wherever they met. On the bus, in the parks, on the playgrounds, persons would recognize them and express their hopes to them. Katherine and Jan had started writing down names and addresses of such folk. They'd sent occasional newsletters to this network of people, all parents with a yearning for peace. Being a devout Christian, Jan would ask others to pray for them and the peace initiative. She sensed a worldwide chain of prayer as well.

All of that was enriching, but what about the negotiations themselves? Had their presence had any impact? It was hard to say. The heads of state were greeted by mothers at the beginning of every reconvened session, and the children did skip in for their daily moment of play with these important men.

Beyond that, there had been only the most occasional moment to indicate that anyone noticed their presence or that it made a difference. Once, Natasha and Billy had been drawing pictures on the floor while a tense acrimonious debate raged. At a moment of high tension,

Natasha burst out in tinkling, melodic laughter at something Billy had drawn. The negotiators had looked startled, then starting laughing also. It seemed to Jan that tension broke and that they then proceeded in a more reasonable way.

There was another time. It was a late afternoon. Children squirmed on mothers' laps while participants wearily plodded through innumerable details. A leader spoke up to say the babies needed a nap and so did they. Folks agreed to recess till the next morning, when they tackled the same problem with more vigor and intentionality—or so it seemed to Jan.

Beyond that, Jan was not aware of any direct influence they had exerted. Still, what had she expected? She was pleased to note that for whatever reasons, the talks had moved forward. The plan that had evolved was more bold in its provisions for arms reductions than most had thought possible. Significant concessions had been made on both sides and among the various factions in both countries.

And now the process was almost over. They gathered once more in December. There were a few details to settle. Then there would be a formal signing. Hopefully this would all transpire so that they would have time to be home for Christmas.

The final sessions proceeded with very few problems. Respect and trust had developed between the negotiators. With weary eagerness they ironed out remaining issues. There would be one more session with brief formalities and then signing of this document on which they all had worked so long.

Both mothers had prepared their children that this was to be a very important day and that it would be their last time at the peace talks. Dressed in their very finest, they were in their places in plenty of time. When the heads of state appeared, both children skipped off to greet their favorites. As Jan watched Billy, her heart jumped to her throat. What was that black object in his hand? Oh, God no, not a gun! At the same moment the security guard saw it. Reacting quickly, he threw himself on the child and shouted "Drop it!" Billy screamed and burst into tears as it fell to the floor. Another guard rushed to help. He picked up the object and saw that it was a plastic toy gun.

Jan knelt beside her child. "I'm so sorry," she said. "I don't know where this came from. He's not even allowed to play with toy guns."

Billy piped up, "It was my prize from David's birthday. I was going to give it to Uncle Nicki to make him laugh."

The guard examined it carefully and then handed it to the Russian leader. He pointed it to the ceiling and squeezed the trigger. It shot a stream of water upward. He laughed a couple of times, as did others, though rather uneasily. "I accept your gift, Billy. I have planned a gift for you as well." An assistant brought a box, which he opened for Billy. "Look, child, a big tractor and many things to pull."

Billy said thank you, but he looked confused.

"Don't you understand? Now we can make more tractors and less tanks or missiles. People will eat better because of it." He turned to his assistant, "I think he will like the other gift better." The aide returned with the second gift, a child-sized attaché case, similar to the ones that everyone around the table carried. Billy beamed at this gift. Immediately he carried it and walked around the table, shaking hands with each, as he had watched them do. By now the mood in the room was much less tense. The assistant gave identical gifts to Natasha. The American president had a gift for Natasha. He had observed how she often amused herself with number games. And so he gave her a computerized game to improve math skills. He knelt with her for just a moment to help her get started on it. In fairness, one was given to Billy, also. By now it was time to proceed with the signing ceremony so that all could disperse to their flights for home.

Jan sat there in a state of shock, scarcely noticing what was happening around her. She thought how fragile the search for peace is. In spite of meaning well, her son had almost disrupted it with the gift of a toy gun! All at once, she was startled to realize that it was over, that people were joyously shaking hands, hugging, embracing.

Both mothers rose and guided their children out through the crowds. The four of them walked down the street together. The children were holding hands and clutching their favorite gifts.

The bells of the churches were all ringing in honor of the peace treaty. As they passed a lovely old church, Jan stopped and asked Katherine if she would mind waiting a moment while she went in to pray.

In the silence of the lovely majestic sanctuary, well-loved Bible readings came to mind, texts she had been hearing in Advent worship. These scriptures flowed over Jan with refreshment: "The wolf shall dwell with the lamb, and the leopard shall lie down with the kid, and the calf and the lion and the fatling together, and a little child shall lead them. . . . They shall beat their swords into plowshares, and their spears into pruning hooks; nation shall not lift up sword against nation, neither shall they learn war any more . . . To us a child is born . . . and his name shall be called . . . Prince of Peace." She prayed simply, "Thank you, God, for such a day. God, please give us peace." Quietly she mused, Grandma, I think we did what you would have wanted. As she rose to leave, she saw Katherine and Natasha kneeling in the back pew, crossing themselves and going out.

They said their good-byes in the hotel lobby. Aware that they had become closer than family itself, this farewell was especially difficult. From now on, their ties would be spiritual, supported by an occasional letter. The four held each other close for a long time. Katherine whispered in Jan's ear, "Don't be sad. Our work is just beginning. All children have a better chance for a future, now. We must continue to help our children grow and serve."

Yes, she thought as she rode to the airport. One chapter is over, another begins. And who knows all that the future holds? Perhaps Natasha will one day be a famous scientist. Maybe Billy will be at those negotiating tables, not as a playing child, but as a committed leader. Somehow, some way, the influence of those children must spread, those children of peace. Yes, it was true—"a little child shall lead them."

JOEY TO THE WORLD

The excitement that Joe and Meredith Owens had felt just a few months ago—where had it gone? Now the mood was bleak. How thrilled they had been when that call came from the fire chief in Beaver Lake. They were so pleased to learn that Joe was the successful candidate for the vacancy in their department. They accepted the position that very day. Never mind that they would have to move away from Meredith's parents. Her brother and sister had done that, and they kept in touch. Now, with a baby on the way, their first, it would be an adventure to start a new home and life in a new place.

Enthusiastically they had investigated their new community. Eventually, they had found a little home they could afford (with a loan from parents). It needed lots of work, but they could do that. Together they undertook a dozen tasks to make it the way they wanted. First there was patching, painting, and wallpapering. Then there were curtains and drapes; and next shelves, pictures, and hangings. They bought a few trees and lots of shrubs. Over in one corner, they started a little rose garden. They put a couple of climbers on the fence and hoped one day that corner would be a blaze of color. Little by little, their home was becoming what they had hoped it would be.

Whenever they had a few extra dollars, there was another fun task. They loved shopping trips to equip the nursery. Decorating it was a project filled with anticipation.

They had joined a church and made the acquaintance of several people they hoped to get to know better. In August, Meredith's parents had come for a weekend to see them and their new home.

It was after her parents' visit that Meredith began to admit an occasional nudge of discontent. Until her folks were there, she had pushed from her mind how much they had enjoyed an occasional Sunday dinner or evening with them. She and her mom had gone shopping one afternoon during the visit. This also reminded her of a once frequent, special time, now almost never possible. Then too, they missed their old friends from their hometown. These were folks you could drop in on without notice or call and suggest a movie or an evening of cards on a whim. If possible, they'd do such things with you. They hadn't found any folks like that in Beaver Lake.

Meredith's biggest complaint was Joe's work schedule. His department operated on a "two on, one off" schedule. That is, he went in and had to stay for two full twenty-four-hour days. Then he was off one twenty-four-hour day. After that rotation several times over, there was extra time off. That schedule increasingly irritated Meredith. When he was gone, she was so lonely in this strange city without friends. When he was home, she felt smothered and without privacy. It hadn't been so bad in the early months when they both had lots of projects and when the weather was good enough to be outside. Now, whether alone or with Joe, Meredith felt cooped-up and cramped. She was also beginning to feel fat and awkward. She tired easily and became upset at herself for not accomplishing more. Meredith was beginning to hate life in this town.

Joe was having problems of his own. He had very much wanted to be a fire fighter. That had been his dream all his life. He had gone through special training, then tests and interviews in several places. It had taken years finally to be accepted. He had never doubted that if some department accepted him, he'd do fine.

Now he wasn't so sure. He liked the work and some of the team of fire fighters, but he wasn't sure they liked him. He was well aware that in this department, every new person was on a six-month probationary trial. He felt no confidence that he would be put on permanent status.

Joe kept hearing about folks who dropped out because their family couldn't take the schedule. He wondered if he would be such a dropout. He thought that his work was probably OK, but he wasn't sure, since no one ever told him how he was doing. He wondered where he and Meredith would be when his six-month trial period was up.

The latter weeks of November and the early ones of December were cold and bitter. At the Owens's, the mood inside the house matched the weather outside. They were tense, and, for the first time in their marriage, not even civil with each other. Back in better times, he had loved to call her "Merry, Merry," and she would call him "Pal Joey." They hadn't offered those names to each other for a long time. Previously, they loved to have little pretend arguments that would stretch on and on. Though others did not always understand, it was just one of their ways of being playful. Lately, such kidding hadn't worked. One would snap back or be hurt. The game would go sour.

When he had a spare moment at work, Joe found himself brooding and worrying about his problems with Meredith. He felt so out of step with her right now. He reflected that when he and Meredith went dancing, once in a while he'd lose the rhythm of the music. They'd stop, and in a moment start over again. It seemed to him that they had both lost the rhythm of living and of loving each other. Neither seemed to know how to stop and get in step again.

Then, as if things weren't bad enough, two blows occurred on the same day. One was a letter from her parents saying that since they would be visiting after the baby came, they would be going to Sis's house for Christmas. The other blow was Joe's work schedule. He was required to work both on Christmas Eve and on Christmas Day.

Joe and Meredith had each been secretly hoping for a miracle at Christmas. Both were persons of faith and in need of help. Somehow they had clutched at the possibility that sharing Christmas would help them get themselves together, rekindle their love, and help them realize what really matters. Now that was denied them. Each would be spending Christmas—for the first time in a lifetime—alone!

The dreaded morning of December 24 arrived. Joe had to leave for work or be late, and he wanted no black marks on his record. He said, "We don't have to be in the same place to be with each other."

"You're right," Meredith answered. Both lied.

She said, "This won't be so bad. Christmas is whenever we can be together. The twenty-sixth will be fine."

Joe responded, "That's true." Both lied a second time.

"Will you be OK?"

"Yes, will you?"

"Yes." With the third lie, an awkward hug, and a halfhearted kiss, he was gone.

Meredith's Christmas Eve day didn't go quite as badly as she had feared. She cleaned house, baked a little, and took a nap. Though it was cold and slippery, she risked driving to the Christmas Eve pageant. The program was OK, except she hated going alone—it seemed to her that everyone else was with family. As soon as it was over, she quickly slipped away and drove home.

When she entered the house, it was quiet and lonely.

She put a stack of Christmas records on the player, but their sentimental sounds intensified her loneliness. She turned it off. Paging through the TV guide, she decided against any of the Christmas specials. Those should be watched next to someone you love. How about finishing those last Christmas cards? No, every one carried a memory and distance from someone she loved. She'd rather not think about that tonight. Another batch of cookies? No, she thought, I don't want to do that by myself. And I certainly don't want to fill this house with baking smells just for me. I guess I may as well go to bed, although I'm not tired. Maybe if I read a little. . . .

At that moment, Meredith was given something else to think about. A sharp pain shot through her abdomen tarrying for nearly a minute and then leaving her. Thoroughly frightened, she dialed the fire station and asked for Joe. "He's gone. They all are. Big fire out at the Valley Mobile Home Park. With the wild shifting winds, they're going to have their hands full. I doubt if I can reach him even in an emergency. Is this an emergency?"

"No, I don't think so, net yet," Meredith stammered and hung up.

She sat, waiting. The pains erratically returned from time to time, sometimes milder, sometimes stronger. About midnight the pains became more regular and persistent. She called the fire station once more. Joe was still unreachable, but the dispatcher promised to find help. Very shortly her doorbell rang. LeDell Biggs, a friendly, competent mother of four and wife of a veteran fireman, stood at the door. "Our husbands are working at their job together, let's work at ours," LeDell suggested with a smile.

And so they did. They talked and drank tea, timed labor pains, alerted obstetrician and hospital. A few hours later LeDell assured her it was time. She drove a warmed car to her back door and took Meredith the short drive to their hospital.

Even then this new friend stayed with her. She told her she was doing fine and assured her that the birth was not far away. She was close at hand when the first cries of a baby girl were heard. After a few words of congratulations and praise, LeDell was on her way.

By now Meredith was ready to lean back and rest. But not quite yet. She heard a familiar, excited voice in the hall. Then with sterile gown hastily thrown on, he burst through the door. "What's the idea of going ahead without me?"

"Joe, are you OK?"

"Sure, fine. I think I did my part tonight. We rescued a family with two small children. They'll be OK, though they breathed a lot of smoke." She could smell the smoke when he came near. "The captain let me ride the ambulance to see you for a few minutes. Where's my. . . ." At this moment a nurse appeared, carrying their daughter. Joe's eyes filled with wonder as he reached out to hold their firstborn child. Then he gingerly sat on the bed next to Meredith, that they might hold her together. Joe tried to say something, but his eyes and throat were full. For once, there was an event so awesome, that even he was speechless. Finally he whispered, "Oh Merry, Merry."

Eventually, Meredith broke the silence. "Do you know what I want to name her? I want to name her after her brave daddy who was rescuing other children the very moment she was born." This stirred the clown in Joe, and he began humming melodramatic music and moving, rocking his daughter in a gentle dance. Meredith smiled and continued, "I want to name her Joey."

Joe quickly responded, "Joy, that's a nice Christmas name."

Meredith shouted, "Joey, you dope, not joy." The baby reacted, opening her eyes and shutting them, unafraid.

Joe went on, "Let's see, what was that other name you liked? Hephzibah? Yes, that's it. Joy Hephzibah! I'll fill in the birth certificate when I leave."

Meredith giggled, "Before you go with that stupid name, hold us for a little longer."

The three cuddled together in the closest of embraces. The rhythm was back. The miracle of Christmas!

"You know, Joe," Meredith said to her husband, "before, the birth of Jesus was just a story. Now I've experienced it—the loneliness, the pain, the fear, the kindness of others. How much God risked to give us that child and this one. God was in that birth and this one."

Joe nodded in agreement and then reluctantly rose. "Merry, I must go. The ambulance crew is waiting. We don't have to be in the same place to be with each other."

"Any time we're together is Christmas. The twenty-sixth will be just fine."

"You OK?"

"Yes, are you?"

"Yes."

This time they did not lie. With an unawkward hug and a wholehearted kiss, he was on his way.

Meredith carried Joey to the window and looked out. From her third story view, she saw an incredibly beautiful world of white snow on a clear blue night, Christmas lights twinkling, the first hints of dawn in the east. She watched the lights and exhaust of the ambulance as it drove off.

She was now ready to trust her baby to the nurse's care and have a good, deep sleep. Before she did, however, she offered her Christmas prayer. She lifted up the baby in exultation, then humbly bowed, as she said, "Joey to the world. The Lord has come! Amen."

About the Author

Richard P. Olson is senior pastor of Prairie Baptist Church in Prairie Village, Kansas. He holds the Ph.D. in social ethics and sociology of religion from Boston University and received degrees in New Testament and New Testament Theology from Andover Newton Theological School. He received a bachelor of arts degree in speech/drama and sociology from Sioux Falls College.

The author has served churches in Colorado, Wisconsin, Massachusetts, and South Dakota. He has taught sociology, religion, ethics, and pastoral theology courses and has led workshops on midlife, life planning, remarriage, teaching the Bible, guiding youth in vocational decisions, and sexuality.

The author's previously published works include: *Ministry With Families in Flux, Help for Remarried Couples and Families, Changing Male Roles in Today's World,* and *Mid-Life: A Time to Discover, A Time to Decide.*

The author is an enthusiast for the arts in the church. "I believe that we have a message to proclaim that is so majestic, it is inexpressable," he says. "The arts—particularly music, drama, and story—help us communicate that message that is beyond words."